RHAPSODY OF A HERMIT

RHAPSODY OF A HERMIT

AND THREE TALES BY

MICHAEL ROTHSCHILD

THE VIKING PRESS NEW YORK

"The Austringer" originally appeared in *The Paris Review,* and "Dog in the
Manger" originally appeared in *Antaeus.* "The Price of Pine" originally ap-
peared in *Works in Progress.*

To Catharine

CONTENTS

THE
AUSTRINGER

1

A taut woman, Edith Leon was of necessity a methodical woman. She could not abide the world to float about her as it chose. Mysteries, ambiguities, tormented her. So she retaliated. She marshaled the world into patterns. She embraced a System. First-born was Theory, but soon after came Idea, and lastly, Perception. The world ceased to float. The world was fixed, coherent, sensible as a bucket brigade from a cistern.

Gestures, words, pictures, art—all became clues, surrogates, flares lit by the troubled in their darkness for those who could translate . . . so concluded Edith Leon, formerly college student of psychology, now translator of events, wife of Walter Leon, a clothier, and mother of Warren, a clever and disturbing young doodler.

Once, she had gathered together Warren's abandoned high-school texts, margins littered with grinning birds about to kill, killing, or having killed grinning fish. In a small black booklet concealed in a dresser beneath Warren's socks and underwear she later unearthed a sequence resembling the hieroglyphs of an ancient ceremonial tomb. Page after page was populated by a breed of men whose foreheads sloped without indentation to acutely angular nosetips. Most of the faces were drawn in profile. Lips were singularly thin with downward turns at the mouthcorners. Eyes were ovoid and large, encasing circular uncolored pupils. The eyes lacked brows and lashes. But the most shocking particular was their martial helmets—falcons with dark lizard eyes peered over human heads until headpiece fused to head and falcons nested in human brains.

A mutation resulted toward the end of Warren's booklet. The fine skull structures of the men broadened; their noses coarsened and hooked down, eclipsing their thin lips. Their rounding eyes blackened and shone from either side of a strongly cleft curling beak. The headdress had become the head and it sat on a thick-ribbed human trunk.

Bristling with evidence, Edith Leon brought the drawings to her husband. The fact that Warren drew pictures pleased Walter Leon from the start. He owned a garment shop for ladies and alone fashioned its window displays. The den, a square wooden caboose coupled to their brick house, was of his design. To his specifications the rich wood had been tongue-and-grooved, he had chatted supervisions to a plodding carpenter over his own blueprints, and afterwards spent early evenings reclined in his creation, scanning garment bulletins beneath a sunken ceiling beam. That Warren drew pictures was natural.

Edith insisted they were *abnormal* pictures. Her hazel eyes flagging urgency and a paucity of iodine, she unraveled what she deemed her son's "fanatical hatred of fish and fowl." As proof of and perhaps antidote to his malady, they would purchase animals, install animals in their house, and observe Warren's responses. She had decided to purchase two goldfish and one parakeet.

Edith watched, but Warren took little notice of the racket issuing from the wire-bell birdcage or the goldfish bowl set on the television beside the miniature cactus. She did her best to give the fishbowl appeal. Besides the two fish Edith anchored a gray ceramic castle and deep-sea diver in an inch of smooth chartreuse, purple, and blue pebbles.

Nonetheless, Warren declined to feed the fish. Daily the fish rose to the tiny flakes Edith salted on the surface of the water. Warren refused to watch the fish. Each day Edith sat for a time before the bowl while the fish hung in the water waving their tails, their mouths opening and closing. The bowl became gray, and meandering strings of white excrement trailed the fish. In an effort to clean the murky bowl, Edith dumped the water down her kitchen sink. The fish hopped from the poured water, eluded her net, and were lost flipping and slapping in the well of her grinding garbage disposal.

The parakeet fared better. Edith named the turquoise and yellow bird Cuckoo and elaborately outfitted his cage with diversions and obstacles: bells of seed, ringing bells, wooden and plastic perches, oblong beak sharpeners, mirrors, a ladder, a removable sandpaper floor for droppings, a snowman with spring legs for butting and an embroidered gauze blanket to ease the darkness—Cuckoo wanted nothing. Edith spent hours talking to the bird as he bobbed before a mirror and picked his perch. Gradually his random chirps, yells and squawks abated and a limited but intelligible jabber emerged. Cuckoo bid Edith good morning and evening and all the day said "prettypretty" in a high voice.

Late evenings there was silence intermittently splintered by the shrill fixed voice of the parakeet. Edith slept in the den, pale in the spotlight of the ceiling beam. Cuckoo perched on her collarbone, his head cocked to the side, quizzically. Edith's lids masked her eyes into coyness. There they slept, Edith's eyes ajar slightly, Cuckoo's purple lids perfectly sealed.

Had Edith Leon been a sibyl as well as a translator of events and seen Warren hunched over an attic desk in the cricket-ridden country night of future years, had she seen his desk piled with books entitled *Birds of Prey*, *The Misunderstood Raptores*, *The Noble Art*, *Hawking for You*, and *The Complete Falconer*, and known that he had a doeskin gauntlet, a rawhide-wrapped metal perch, and lacked nothing but a hawk, she would have celebrated the confirmation of her System, her Theories, her Ideas, and her Perceptions.

And had she known her son's rapture as he perused his maroon drawing book (particularly the entries he imagined to resemble a sequined lady releasing herself from the trapeze, somersaulting in the air and at the last moment clutching the steel forearms of a gent in caramel-colored tights), how jubilant her own celebration would have been: a speck hangs high on the top of Warren's page; below a dun partridge flushes from a green copse. The speck enlarges, a falcon banks, surveying, and dives, its wings pulled tight, unclear for its speed, like a comet. In a brown circle of detached quills the smaller predator penetrates the partridge with hooked hands clenched, binds to, and drops the stunned bird, watching its graceless tumbling descent. On the ground the blackheaded falcon rests on the brown body, dips its toothed beak, and with an abrupt twist, unlinks two neck vertebrae. The sharp wings of the falcon encircle the partridge breast, mantling. Again the black head dips, depluming the short tan chest feathers. Cleaned, the breast meat is white and prickled. The final picture shows the falcon straddling the vermilion bird, a thick neck, crop packed with the whiteness of breast meat—had Edith Leon but an inkling such acrobatics were to be performed in her son's brain she should have leapt from the sofa tousling her short gray hair and fixed her turbid eyes on the mantic black eyes of her parakeet. Understanding, the bird would have fattened his brindled gorge and chanted, "morbidWarrenmorbidWarrenmorbidWarren," with the toxic roteness of a conscience.

2

Warren courted Gretel throughout the snowstorms, sleet, hail, sun, and warm downpour of March, wooing her with sketches of her naked torso. She posed on a stool between the silver-painted radiator and the gas stove, her toes curled around the dowel supporting the stool legs. Sometimes she wrapped a fuchsia-and-gray-banded blanket around her waist and goosefleshed thighs. She fanned her arms and undulated her body, embellishing the description of her day: the expedition to the toilets where little girls flapped their arms and were angels, the little boys sidewinding beside in a separate line, miming snakes. How

Denise may or may not have stolen Randy's milk dime. Crystal's right eye swollen shut.

Gretel's wavy brown hair filled the deep V scoops between her collarbone and neck, hanging down her pale back in uneven lengths. Her breasts seemed larger for the fineness of her ribcage. Balanced on a dark but sparse line of down, her navel protruded slightly and the tips of her jutting pelvis deepened the grooves that outlined her pubic crest.

She liked the way Warren concentrated, whisking a charcoal stick over his large tablet or pausing to rub the stick on sandpaper and blow away black powder; his irritation in rolling a caramel block of eraser on an errant line until gray twists cluttered the floor.

Art school was teaching Warren an architectured human body —how the skull was a dome capping clavicles and scapulae which provided awning for the rotunda of ribbery; how the pelvis (secondary supports) snugly socketed balled pillars, the whole resting upon the arches of the feet. With the mind of his studies Warren erected queer and gabled human buildings. He rubbed his lines into what he called "shadow studies," blurred to the degree his pages appeared spat upon and licked. Once charcoaled in his sketch pad, Gretel's ruddy nipples became dead as cigar ashes; her torso the same that hung from wire and stocked shelves and tables of his studio classroom—plaster of Paris trunks of classical statuary.

Dissatisfied, Warren avoided his lectures. He skipped studio instruction. His pictures only changed—and changed abruptly— the first of April when Gretel blandly said, as if describing the daffodil sachet her principal, Mrs. Winkeller, stashed in the right side of her bosom, that she was not having her periods.

The chiaroscuro human building of his studies began to quake. Construction blocks that dunked, twisted, and tilted on sagittal, horizontal and transverse planes split, crumbled. Like a child who in play has so earnestly erected a castle of wooden blocks, Warren, with one sweeping blow toppled the spires and turrets, cleaved the pyramidal base of the classroom thumb from the balled middle, cleaved the balled middle from the pear-shaped tip, and like a child, found more mirth in the collapse than the construction. Secretly he purchased a box of crayons and with bright primary colors roped by fat black lines, started Gretel's pregnancy.

For five days he made pictures of the changes he supposed her childbearing would manifest. As the red embryo enlarged, her stomach skin stretched taut and blued. At the last Warren drew the bulge as something discrete; sometimes a fantastic saffron balloon or a transparent globe veined with waterways, whitish land masses, oceanic; sometimes buffed, a mirrored sphere reflecting the sky, the silver bars of the radiator. The fifth day a delivery was imminent. The navel had popped out long and straight like the stem of a great hard blue fruit.

At night Warren's fingertips tested her unchanging nipples, his palm alert for wetness. His ear, cradled between her hips, listened to the snaps and squeals of her digestion. He bought newspapers and analyzed the classified sections. He scanned job opportunities and realized he did not know how to do anything. He tried to imagine a distributor cap. Through green goggles he saw his hands solder together pieces of copper tubing, stitch uppers to shoe soles, adjust the floating balls in backs of toilets. One morning a week before Gretel's kindergarten classes ended he went so far as to introduce Warren Leon, window stylist, to Mr. Ransom, proprietor of the Swallow Shop.

Ransom told Warren he had done it himself once a week for fourteen years. He pressed his flattened palm on the speckled tie over his breastbone and said his heart was the reason. He led Warren through a drab green-curtained dressing room in the back of his shop, down stairs into a dim basement, a long corridor with small perpendicular recesses. The cellar walls were brick and fieldstone chinked and patched with concrete. The air was damp and water trickled between the black stones. Ransom pointed out a workbench to the right backed with shelves of odd tools and spattered paint cans. They passed the alcove of the boiler, toilet-paper and light-bulb closet.

The prop room was at the remote end of the cellar. The props were in crates and boxes marked by seasons. Ransom said his summer merchandise had arrived and that Warren should "center on brights." Together they would coordinate the summer windows and display cases. What they needed, explained Ransom, was a bouncy summer panorama—all McIntosh red, grapefruit yellow, and tangerine. "Geared" to lure people in off the wet streets for a taste of summer. He coughed into a paisley handkerchief and left Warren alone in the basement with the crates containing the seasons of the year.

Warren opened an enormous box marked A U T U M N. It was stuffed with picket fences, vines of red and yellow leaves, a blackboard announcing "Back to School Days" and a brilliant orange and green plastic pumpkin. Under the leaves Warren saw a rigid brown hook. He dislodged the hook which became the tail of a brown Airedale dog with a broken ear and a scarlet collar and leash.

Placing the dog aside, he opened S U M M E R. It contained fishnets, opaque green and red glass bubbles, sanddollars, seashells, and fragile crab bodies. A second box was layered with bathing caps growing soft rubber flora, scaled bathing caps, and sandals. The brown, red, gold, and black hairpieces and wigs beneath, shiny and coarse, blanketed a tangle of legs and fingers. The hands were poised to offer a harlequin scarf, a beaded handbag with a yellow flower. One of the legs was chipped and revealed a wire bone. Another had been repainted on the calf with an orange in uncomfortable contrast to the pink-fleshed original. The bald lower half of a mannequin, its right buttock impaled on the metal shaft of a stand, rose out of a red-berried holly wreath in the W I N T E R crate.

Warren never returned to the Swallow Shop from his first lunch hour. In a glass cubicle around the corner he phoned Walter Leon long-distance to secure a large check for the summer. From the booth he jogged the entire way to Maple Street School. There, through the chicken-wired window of a door, befuddled Warren was watching Gretel chalk H and h above rows of tiny heads when a grimacing squat woman, overwhelming with the odor of daffodils, eyes ever-alert for a molester, asked aggressively, "Mister, are you looking for someone?" Warily, "Excuse me . . . Mister, can I help you?"

3

From the attic space serving as his studio/study Warren surveyed his rented domain. Behind the farmhouse twenty or so acres of thistle and witchgrass tangled to a blighted elm in the ravine. He could not see beyond the firtops behind a knoll of pine seedlings planted in rows, but after her hike Gretel reported that the meanders of a stream, high from the rainy June and tawny from the pulp mill in Starks, described the far boundary of their land.

Much as he began it, Warren concluded his first week of country life—gazing across the field through the tortuous branches of the elm. This elm towered so foolishly barren amidst the lush ravine, so gloomily contrived with the plump raven squatting on the remains of a limb, that Warren devised through its branches the busyness of a Brueghel winterscape: on the knolltop he set a kerchiefed woman to collect faggots; in the left foreground weary hunters waded through drifts of snow; sharp-chested hounds poked their muzzles into snow crust near a fire; the ravine was a frozen canal where boys played hockey.

Suddenly one incongruous boy braved the chill dressed in a striped green and yellow jersey. He ambled down the knoll of seedlings, across the skating canal and vanished behind the elm trunk. His torso emerged from the ravine, arms waving away Warren's winterscape, waving up at Warren in the window.

Hurriedly Warren turned from the window. His back parallel

to the slope of the hewn roof timbers, he moved to his desk by the brick chimney cutting through the attic floor. He opened the great maroon drawing book. With quick flicks of his pencil he scattered sharp-angled bird and fish shapes over the page. The fish were rudimentary, much like capital Ys fallen on their side or else snatched from the alphabet by primitive birds whose heads contained a broad parabolic grin. It was apparent the birds felt quite correct impaling the fish and the fish had no misgivings in being killed by such birds.

Voices and the splutter of an engine lured Warren back to the window. Gretel was pacing out the size of her garden plot below in giant steps. A bald man astride a quivering rust-orange tractor concurred by nodding his corded neck. The boy in the striped green and yellow jersey leaned on a glacial boulder nearby and watched. His stiff reddish hair covered his forehead and shaded his beaked nose. Perhaps he was twelve or thirteen. Gretel completed the outline and piled her thick brown hair on her head to catch the breeze on the back of her neck. A sleeveless ruby shell molded her unbridled breasts into the gentlest curve. The boy sat cross-legged in the sun chewing a blade of grass, his back against the boulder.

The wedged blade dropped and the machine traced Gretel's steps, turning up heavy overlapping lines of black earth. The plowman was exceedingly serious and neat. He checked his progress behind. Shortly a small dark rectangle was notched in the gnarled field. The farmer stopped the noise of his engine and walked stiffly up to Gretel. He squatted, picked up some dirt, and for a quarter of an hour all Warren managed to intercept were the fragments: "sure to crop your tomato suckers," "three to a hillock," "nothin' like bloodmeal," and a preening invitation to "come see my pigeonhouse." The boy rose to join them, his arms folded on his chest. The farmer laughed (how pointless, causeless, laughter appears from a distance, scowled Warren from one window corner), daubed his neck with a blue sheet of a handkerchief, and remounted his machine. He aimed his tractor at Warren, idled, and shouted over his engine to Gretel, "Don't expect too much the first time. It'll be a lot better next year when all this rots. I'll be by to harrow in the mornin'," and he steered his jolting machine over the clotted field to the road.

Gretel squinted up at the attic, her hands curved along the lines of her dark eyebrows. It was too late for Warren to remove his head from behind the window frame. "Warren, come outside." The boy smiled widely into the lowering sun. "A minute," said Warren. He slanted past the chimney toward the stairway, paused at the top of the stairs to gather himself, and descended.

"This is Anthony," Gretel said. "He wants to know if we have any odd jobs for him." Anthony sat on the pepper-speckled granite porch steps and examined Warren. Incest, decades of inbreeding, finally produced such eyes, thought Warren. Wide rubberoid lids concealed half Anthony's eyes, giving the impression of an ocular drift into the forehead, a fear the boy was about to swoon or was preparing a backward somersault.

With index finger and thumb of his right hand Anthony kneaded some flesh on the left underside of his chin, his head cocked to one side. He scanned the shabby lawn and said, "Looks like you wanna have your lawn mowed. I mow lawns, you know."

"No, I didn't," said unhappy Warren trying to lift his mouth-corners into an inquisitive yet sympathetic smile.

"I do," said Anthony flatly.

"Do you have a lawnmower?"

"Nope,"

"Well, I don't have one."

Anthony eyed Warren, shrugged, hung his left hand over his right shoulder and walked down the driveway to the road, scratching his shoulder blade.

Warren sensed Gretel was now sucking her soft inner lips tight to her long incisors in her conception of a glare. The looks she gave him! He had first glimpsed her lips' enviable gift of contortion when she brought Crystal, a sullen red-haired five-year-old, into their apartment. Clamped under Gretel's arm was a stack of finger-paintings by her kindergarten children. Crystal and Gretel proceeded to thumbtack his olive kitchen into a crazy quilt. Warren had scuttled into the bedroom and closed the door. Together Gretel and Crystal looked at the pictures and talked about cows, gardens, chickadees, and cats. Wearied of listening behind the door, Warren opened it a slit and beheld Gretel and Crystal spooning flesh-colored chunks from a carton of peach ice cream. Gretel had raised her eyes and of a sudden, cinched her mouth into a miraculous spasm of triumph, antagonism, repulsion, willfulness, and cold ice cream.

This face in particular Warren remembered. He sat on the steps and fingering the warm granite said, "What did you want me to do?" He looked up for an answer and saw Gretel's back, arms akimbo, hands girding her waist, retreating to the garden. "He didn't even have a lawnmower," reasoned Warren.

Gretel straddled a black corrugation of earth, bowed, and commenced throwing stones and mats of turf outside the garden's perimeter. She tugged at an obdurate root when Warren shouted, "Do you want to abort right in the middle of the garden?" Without turning, Gretel shot her right arm erect in an obscene gesture, reclutched the root, and with a heave wrenched it from the ground.

⟞§ She had been too busy to notice the dusk. Catching herself on her knees, feeling the garden in darkness for rocks, Gretel laughed softly through her nose. The clouded moon was nearly full circle. Except for the amber rectangle of the attic window, the farmhouse was gray against the moving black clouds. She straightened, arched, and pressed her thumb-pads into the knotted small of her back. Before her like a colossal antler, the black elm pronged the sky. She sauntered toward the farmhouse alternately kneading and drumming her back with her knuckles.

Far up the road she heard the approaching drone of a truck. A pale beam of light curved into the night. Just before the logging truck rumbled past she sighted the silhouette of a bicyclist pedaling along the opposite roadside. Momentarily, Anthony was washed in the truck's headlights, one hand on a fringed handlebar, the other hanging lax by his thigh. In the scarlet of the truck's wake both his hands gripped the streaming handlebars. He was pedaling strenuously, his buttocks pumping off the seat, his neck extended low. The truck shifted gears and Gretel watched it return Anthony to an umbra racing the shadows of the roadside. A fine rain sounded pleasantly to Gretel as it pricked the grass. The wind blowing from the knoll of seedlings strengthened.

Gretel went inside and paused by the shed entrance. Warren paced the attic. She slipped into the bathroom and closed the door. A shiny disc of metal nailed above the porcelain washstand (a peephole of a mirror discouraging all but the piecework of shaving and hair tweezing) reflected the reddish-brown smudges highlighting Gretel's cheekbones. Her face had been smeared by her fingertips in the garden, pushing her pesky hair away, fastening it behind her ears. Her bare feet and her hands were stained with dirt. She undressed, turned the spiky shower as hot as she could bear and stepped under it, her chin on her chest, waiting for her muscles to unstring. The doorknob turned and Warren's head popped from behind the plastic shower curtain, smiling vaguely into the humid shower stall. "How do you feel?"

"Sore," said Gretel, twisting water out of her hair. She shut her eyes, threw back her head and let the water bounce off her face and shoulders. Rivulets streaked between her breasts, hung on her belly, and dropped in a steady stream from the pointed hair between her thighs.

"Like a hothouse here," offered Warren. The door reclosed and Gretel began to turn the soapbar in her hands, working a lather.

A hard rain slanting through the open attic window darkened the floor. Warren shut the window and sat idly thumbing through *Birds of Prey and Art*, a tome tracing raptorial art from the petroglyphs of Lascaux through bird-souled Egyptian relics to Tranquillo Cremona's somber canvas "Il Falconiere," or "Love and Jealousy," depicting a woman guardedly resting on a mustachioed picaroon's chest while his irked falcon, uneasily jessed to his raised gloved fist, beats the dusky air around them. Disquieting rain was tinkling steadily on the window glass.

In the steamy bathroom below, Gretel bent over, her stringy wet hair hanging nearly to the linoleum floor. She wrapped a towel around the back of her head and straightened, adroitly fashioning a turban. She rubbed the clouded metal disc to see herself and opened the door. Mist rushed into the kitchen. She wiped the moisture from the bathroom window with her wet towel. Her body felt nicely spent. In the clearing window she held out her arms and gyrated them in small circles, enjoying her turbaned nakedness. Moving closer to the window, she flexed her jaws open and closed. She started. Her face's reflection did not correspond to her face. Anthony's unabashed lidded eyes peered through the streaked glass. His wet hair was matted on his forehead, his sharp nose flattened against the outside glass.

Gretel did not overtly acknowledge him. She powdered herself, unwound the turban and ruffled her hair briskly with a towel. Uneasy, she at last pulled the string overhead, shutting the light off.

Long after midnight Warren slipped into bed beside Gretel who half-turned, murmured, and covered her head with his pillow. He folded his hands over his stomach and readied for the interminable hodgepodge of episodes, unwinding installments "to be continued" after his somnambulant return from the water faucet or the bathroom still faint with Gretel's lilac-scented talc.

He experimented with methods of falling asleep: he aligned his inhalation with sleeping Gretel's; opposed her exhalation with his inhalation; ignored all her night sounds. This failing, he waited for a distant engine noise to mount, braced himself during its brutal climax (its light show skimming across the ceiling and down the wall), and relaxed as it diminished to the sough of Gretel's lungs and unperturbed open mouth.

Finally he dreamed, of a hilltop, of making love on a ferruginous shaggy woman. They trundled over and over, laughing down the slope, hugging through goldenrod and lupine, rolling into the river that appeared below. Together they splashed and whipped the water into excitement. They ran up the hill, hands clasped. Asthmatic Warren paused to powerfully sneeze into a gaudy tiger lily.

Gretel imperiously strode over the hillcrest, heavy with laundry. My children, she said, I will teach you to wash clothes in the old way, pounding dirt away on the stones of the river. Warren scampered himself and his increasingly hirsute lover into the suddenly available and vacant abode of a subterranean animal.

Gretel spotted movement on the hillside. Resplendent in scarlet jacket, golden buttons, and white silk stock shirt, she raised a brass horn to her pursed lips and brayed a metallic ta-ta-ta-ta. Hordes of unkempt dog-faced children, their frothy tongues elongated, charged up the hill. Master of hunt Gretel led the hallooing phalanx while on either side whippers-in Crystal and Anthony flailed the grass.

Sconced deep in their den, the furry succubus massaged Warren's jangled spine to calm him. Gretel glowered one hundred jeering eyes of fifty indignant heads over the hole's edge. Warren turned to his conspiratress. She was gone! Warren was alone.

With the intrepid grin of a conjurer, Warren greeted the vituperative mouths that defined the circumference of the hole. He doffed his posh beaver top hat, ran his index finger around the monogrammed pigskin sweatband, and rapped the inner crown. Waving his outstretched palm over the brim, Warren the Wizard produced by the scruff of its neck a ferruginous fox puppy. At once the puppy's yips and thrashes established Warren's innocence and its own authenticity. A final rallying flourish of Gretel's horn plangently abridged Warren's private cinema.

Outside a horn honked and bleated. The front door slammed. It was noon. The bedroom was dark except for a blue strip of sky between the incompletely drawn green canvas shade and the window sill. The room was damp from the night of rain. Warren resolved to vacate the rumpled bed, extricate himself from his gluey pajama bottoms, dress, and welcome the day.

He pulled on green flannel trousers he had bought especially for the country and his green billiard-cloth shirt. He scratched his stubbled cheeks and walked to the bathroom where in the circular shiny metal, gruesome histrionics accompanied his piston-like toothbrush movement.

No sooner had Warren dropped the flannels to his ankles, lifted his shirt-tongues, and become warmly situated on the horse-shoe of the toilet than a queer-voiced "Hello? Hello?" sounded in the kitchen. Grumpily, Warren hitched his trousers. He opened the door to his own piqued head twinned in the mirrorlike sunglasses that sealed the trespasser's eyes.

"She wants you," said ubiquitous Anthony. "Down to the garden." Wetness darkened his dungarees up to his crotch and his fists were wadded in his pockets.

"Tell her I'll be right down," grumbled Warren. The taciturn intermediary did not budge. "Tell her now," Warren ordered and he slammed himself in the bathroom and doused his face with cold water.

Three curled wisps of cloud, the only marks in the bright sky, raced high above the rotting elm. Gretel was standing beside Anthony, the reddish tip of his cowlick level to the lobe of her ear. They watched the farmer harrow the garden. Rows of tiny wheels masticated the caked ground behind the machine. The wind that blew from the firs over the pine knoll and soaked fields was sharp and cold. Warren swished through the tall wet grass to Gretel's back. Her hair was plaited against her bleached denim jacket, an image of severity to Warren. He nodded to the farmer.

The farmer, no longer civil as from the attic window, wore a red-and-black-checked hunting cap and coat. He jounced sourly in his seat, featureless if not for hispid ears and nostrils.

Warren hauled Gretel by the elbow to a flat glacial boulder at the side of the garden. He began (with despondent intensity) from text: "Inbreeding. The son of his father and his older sister, herself the daughter of her father's first cousin—only such a combination could spawn . . ."

"Dougal's got a bird," interjected Gretel.

"Only an impoverished gene pool could result . . ."

"A goshawk."

"Who the hell is Dougal?" asked Warren, his query draining all impetus from his projected tirade.

Gretel pointed to the farmer, who had shut off his clanking engine and was inspecting the steaming nose of his tractor.

Warren loped across the muddy garden and obliquely, accosted Dougal. "My wife tells me you keep hawks?"

"Nope."

Warren ebbed. Old MacDonald, he thought, was of the same impervious and mutant stock as Anthony. Perhaps an uncle. "You don't have a hawk then?"

"Yep, I do."

Warren sufficiently restrained the impulse to cudgel confused or contrary MacDougal to inquire, "How much will you take for him?"

"Her. And she ain't for sale just yet," said morose and inscrutable Donald, fiddling under the orange hood of his machine.

"I don't understand," confessed Warren.

"Look buddy, that damn gossuck has gone and killed my best show pigeon this mornin'. Got caught up in chicken wire. In a day or two you can have all that's left of her."

"I'll give you twenty-five dollars now."

"Nope."

"At least could I take a look at her?"

"Suit yourself," said Dougal. "I'll be home after I harrow Poulin's late this afternoon."

◄§ Formerly, in his preparations to become a falconer, Warren had wandered far, wrapped in a mantle of sable pelts, cantering a coily Arabian stallion over endless dunes, a hooded peregrine balanced on his sure fist. His perusals of falcon lore had resulted in his creation of a gyral sickle-winged enchanter performing thousands of feet above his head. In the labyrinthine castle Gioja del Colle he had discussed avian pecularities with

Frederick II of Hohenstaufen, the weather best to fly at herons. But now Warren was fixed in his peregrinations, assigned by the *Boke of St. Albans* not to be a King with his Gerfalcon, a Knight with a fierce Saker, not even to be a Squire with his Lanner or the Lady's magical Merlin. Feudal hierarchy cast Warren down, down, halting him a rung below the insipid Young Man with his Tree Falcon. Truly Warren could no longer be termed a falconer at all. He was but a Yeoman, his bird a short-winged hawk.

The Noble Art, a morocco-bound volume by Colonel Humphrey Melmoth, further elucidated: "We usually call a hawker, he who keeps a Goshawk, an *austringer* [from the Fr. *autour*, Lat. *astor, austor*]—certainly not a true Falconer." Warren salvaged only a grim comfort from the frontispiece, a photograph of the dapper uniformed author (a petite goateed man holding a snowy gerfalcon as large as his chest, shoulders, and head).

Such salient data did Warren the Yeoman cull from his books after his gloomy return from Dougal's farm. That night he subdued his anxiety by studiously gleaning goshawk facts in his attic lair. He wrestled the wily stratagems that teemed in his head as to how he might burgle barbaric Dougal's farmhouse, how he might rescue his captive Gos.

The visit to see his hawk had been infelicitous from the start. Vengeful Dougal's beagle, a rotund arthritic dog with a violent temper and underbite, had hobbled up to Warren and quite without warning shredded the left leg of his new flannel trousers. Warren had sought refuge through a paunchy screen door. A wizened woman in a long gingham dress was flattening dough into a circle on the kitchen table. Audaciously, without looking at Warren, she said, "Don't you worry, Poker don't bite."

"Where could I find Mr. Dougal, ma'am?" asked assiduous Warren in his most restrained tones, peeking all the while about the room for hawk traces.

"In the barn," said the woman. The flesh on her arms rolled loosely with her motion.

Warren had located Dougal pitching hay before the serried pink noses of spotted cows. He glanced at Warren and forked on while the big-eyed cows lowed impatiently, intermittently plapping pies of dung into the concrete grooves behind them.

Warren waited for ten minutes. His eyes puffed and watered from the hay and he began to sneeze. Finally Dougal walked up to him and said, "Hay fever? What can I do for you, mister?"

Warren gazed through his tears at distorted Dougal and wheezed incredulously, "About the bird!"

"Oh, you're the gossuck fella," and he walked past Warren toward his house. The gouty dog snarled. Warren hastened after its master into a kitchen where the woman was filling the browned piecrust with a viscous yellow substance. Dougal opened a door in the hall and led Warren down a flight of stairs into darkness.

He pulled a string and a light bulb illuminated the moldy stone-walled cellar with its earthen floor. A giant gray wood furnace radiated a tangle of smokestacks, the tentacles of a galvanized octopus. Dougal ducked his head under an angular stack, walked on a plank around the furnace, and pulled another light cord.

"In here, root cellar," said the farmer, pointing to a wooden door. He opened the door and stood outside. His burly frame filled the jamb. On tiptoe, peeping over Dougal's shoulder, Warren saw the glint of translucent orange eyes. In a silvery flash the bird lunged at unflinching Dougal from an oak chopping block. The hawk came to the end of its nylon tether and jerked to the ground at Dougal's boots. She convulsed. With a din of slapping chaotic wings she flounced over and over, seizured. The bird's brown-brindled ivory chest heaved. One of her wings was awkwardly extended, the other tucked tight.

Just as suddenly as she had bated and convulsed, her spasms subsided. The hawk's torrid eyes grew torpid, filmed by a nictitating membrane. Warren noticed her dome feathers were either frayed or missing. In their place rose a raw chestnut tonsure. Dougal slid the bird into the cellar with a soft kick and shut the door.

"What have you done to her head?" asked Warren to Dougal's calves as he trailed him up the stairs.

"Nothin'."

"Don't tell me you found her that way."

"I found her buttin' her damn empty skull on chicken wire tryin' to get out."

"Why didn't you kill her then?"

"Seems she's doin' that just fine by herself," said Dougal. He hung his cap and hunting coat on points of an antler in the hallway and began to scrub his hands in the kitchen sink. "Well buddy, you seen her."

"This morning you said I could have her. Can I take her now?"

"Come by this time tomorrow," Dougal said, sitting with finality at the wooden table, the morning's newspaper at his elbow.

"Piece of hot pie, mister?" said the kind lady. She held out the finished product. "Custard."

"No, thank you, Missus Dougal. I really should . . ."

"Not Missus," spat Dougal, "Charlotte Dougal, my sister."

Charlotte bowed slightly.

Edging and nodding, Warren backed toward the screen door and sidled coolly by crippled Cerberus into the dusk.

ᴗᔓ Many hours passed before he ceased thumping one wicked bastinado after another on the soles of incestuous Dougal's feet and regained the composure requisite to reading of his goshawk. Twice he walked downstairs to use the bathroom and twice he was rebuffed by Gretel's prolonged occupancy. Persistent pressure this second time led him behind the house, where his strained mind heard phantom footsteps running through the grass; far away a farm dog barked, stopped, and barked again at the echo of its bark.

Through the night Warren drowsily compiled the list of equipment he would have to purchase the next day in Starks:

binoculars

gun

fishing rod
swivel
clothesline
soft leather strips
bells

He scribbled diagrams detailing the conversion of the shed into a draft-free hawkhouse, complete with screen perch and vertically doweled windows. A yawn squeezed tears into the corners of his eyes. The torpor settling over his body seemed to extend to the tip of his pencil. Warren's head swayed. Frizzles of iridescence floated across his drooping lids, his neck hinged his chin flush to his sternum.

His obstinate head jerked erect and Warren was awake, startled by the attic window. Like a Peeping Tom, like his mother's perspicacious eye, a full pocked moon hung centered by the cruciform sash. Warren shuffled to the window. Moonlight blanched a hoarfrost, a spring snowfall over the landscape. He uncoiled the shade.

He was administered immediate and potent sedation by Frederick Landseer's treatise, *The Complete Falconer*. Across the yawn of centuries Landseer wiggled his soporific finger and opined:

> Launch not beyond your depth, unfledged Falconer. The education of a raptore necessitates a labour and a love. I stress, select a bird commensurate with your Learning, your Locale, the the Leisure available to you, and not least, your own Fitness. Verbum Sap.

Warren's head rocked above the bulky and salubrious volume in his lap. He felt the pricking of sleep benumb his thighs.

> To have superior birds, birds that will win honour and pre-eminence in the chase, the Falconer must realize the essentials of an ancient and noble art.
> What qualities must need the aspiring Falconer possess?

He should be of average size. If too tall he will be quickly spent and want dexterity. If too short he will be sudden in his motions.

He ought to be moderately well-fleshed: emaciation is a liability as he will be unable to withstand cold and prolonged toil; neither should he be corpulent for he then will be short of breath and plagued by the sun.

He must be sagacious, with a retentive memory, acute hearing, and keen eyesight.

He must have daring and tenacity to bear the rigours of climbing hill and cliff-side, swimming unfordable waters, pressing through thorny bracken.

He must know how to write the language and keep a diary of his progress.

He must possess a stentorian voice to call over the winds.

He must not sleep heavily for he must check his bird several times nightly and rouse at the slightest irregularity of jingling bells.

Training, correcting, consulting his bird shall be his main pleasure. A Falcon under the management of such a Man will exhibit the greatest mettle and address in chasing prey and do honour to the skill . . .

Warren's head was careened on his right shoulder, *The Complete Falconer* asprawl at his feet, when Gretel snapped up the shade to the overcast morning. Her hair was drawn back with a blue headband. The sun had burned the bridge of her nose fire pink. On the metal tray she held was a glass of orange juice and a cup of coffee. Warren contracted his face into a wince.

"Why didn't you come down? Warren, are you mad at me?"

"I have a stiff neck," he said, looking from the gray room into the gray layers of sky. "What a miserable day."

Gretel placed the tray on the floor. "How are you coming with Dougal?"

"He's a butcher."

"He was awfully nice about the garden. He wouldn't take a penny." She walked to the head of the stairs. "Oh, I'm going to hire Anthony to help me plant and weed the garden, things the way they are," she smiled quickly.

"How can you bear those eyes of his, my god, a basilisk . . ."

"Ssssh," sounded Gretel. She pointed down the stairwell.

"I'm going into Starks this morning. Make a list if you want anything." Warren stood and stretched.

"Is that all, basilisks and butchers?" she whispered and skipped down the stairs. Warren fumbled for something apt but already her dark head had disappeared through the floor.

At the kitchen table, while Gretel listed various seed packets, bulk seed, plant sets, and tools, Warren asked Anthony what grade he was in. Anthony took a swallow of milk, aimed his ravaging nonplus at Warren, and erased his fuzzy chalk-colored mustache with a curling swipe of his tongue. "Seventh."

"You're about to enter the eighth?"

"Seventh," said Anthony. He took another swallow of milk.

"Milk and eggs," rescued Gretel and she penciled them beneath "six tomato plants."

&§ The sun burned behind a dense cloud covering, flecking the ash sky with blue, silver, and red. Warren drove into the malodorous village of Starks, crossing the concrete bridge over the Starks River. Under the ledge of sky the river appeared motionless, like livid sheets of rock. Starks was ruled by the wee triumvirate toothpicks, popsicle sticks, and tongue depressors. Suitably, three monolithic stacks were each diademed with columns of royal-blue smoke.

At Jink's Hardware an old man with a crew cut of white spikes sold Warren a cheap green plastic fishing rod and reel, a .22 rifle and ammunition, field glasses, a swivel, a clothesline, packets of seed, tomato and onion sets, a hoe, and a rake.

"Varmints botherin'?" he asked Warren, who could make

neither head nor tail of his intention. "Chucks? Coons?" he yelled as Warren barged out the door.

A permanently smiling matron who spoke no English sold him some supple maroon leather and saddle soap at Mike's Shoe Repair. On the counter a pair of off-white baby shoes had aluminum bells through their laces. Warren pointed to the bells and asked if he could purchase them; if perhaps she had another she might sell. From behind the counter the woman produced a pair of bell-less chocolate-colored boy's shoes. Warren wagged his head from side to side and shook the bells on the off-white infant's shoes. The jovial woman studied a tag on the shoes and said, "Mart-in, Mar-tin."

Warren entered the Five-and-Ten-Cent Store. They stocked cowbells, catbells, deskbells, parakeet bells, and bells for the bedsides of the invalid. "The kind on a baby's laces," Warren explained to the neckless teen behind the glass candy counter.

Warren was on his way out when he spied amidst a heap of orange dolls, astronauts, and black bears, a tiny rubber man with a green silk shirt and a ruby coxcomb. Threaded to the peak of the coxcomb were three round aluminum bells and the reasonable price: seventy-nine cents.

&§ In the yellow circle of Dougal's flashlight beam the lackluster hawk hunched in the root-cellar corner. The lined wooden crate Warren had constructed to transport his goshawk was hardly necessary. Her round bulging eyes had sunken and become oval. A discharge issued from her nostrils and her wings shuddered.

"Instead of friggin' with this bird I'd help out my wife with that garden if I was you," said Dougal.

"You're certainly not, though," said Warren.

"Suit yourself, buddy." Dougal cut the nylon cord around the bird's leg with his pocket knife. Warren, pinioning both her wings, set the hawk into the crate. She did not struggle.

Warren inspected the hawk closely when he had returned to his shed. Her feathers showed hunger traces and were soiled a pasty white around the vent. Her right leg was swollen and discolored where the nylon had eaten into it.

Warren took the attic stairs three steps to a bound. He rummaged through his books for some antidote but they were incomprehensible, archaic. Landseer coruscated over his crucible as he intoned:

> Take a piece of gumdragon; the oil of earthworms and roe, with eels cut in pieces and dipped in warm sheep's blood: mix with incense and mummy . . .

Warren clapped the book shut and downstairs rifled through the medicine cabinet. He decided to paint eucalyptus oil on his hawk's nares with the cotton nub of an ear cleaner and lacquer iodine on her misshapen leg.

Gretel was alone eating at the table when he rushed in for food. He brought the hawk two strips of raw steak on a dish and set it by her side. "Here, Gos," coaxed Warren, dangling the meat before her beak. She looked askance. Warren plopped the meat back on the dish and with assuring measured movements, left the room.

Gretel was rinsing her dinner plate in the sink. "Well, what's the diagnosis?"

"I don't know. She looks terrible."

"She?" said Gretel. She magnified the arch of her brows. "I'm going in to see her, okay?"

"No," said Warren, "I want to see if she eats. Besides, I read that some hawks get riled in a woman's presence."

"Bullshit."

"You can read it for yourself."

Gretel put Warren's supper on the table without comment. She leaned against the stove. "We planted the squash, the carrots, and the beets."

"Ah, that's what seems so odd, madame," simpered Warren. "Where is your catamite?"

"Don't always jeer," said Gretel. "This afternoon while you were in Starks I screwed Anthony. He has no navel. Would you believe it?"

The hillock of mashed potatoes. The peas in a green hump. Seared meat halfway to his mouth, Warren looked up at her bright watchful and mischievous eyes until he had contained himself. He clinked his fork to the plate and said squeakily, "Fine sport for an expectant mother."

Gretel was furious. "That, thank God, I'm not!" she shouted. Her flushed cheeks pulsing, she twirled and dashed from the room.

Warren stayed at the table. He squeezed the mashed potatoes through his fork tines into intricate crinkles around the lip of the plate. He sat at the table until his plate became unfocused. Gos was his single alternative: he rose and walked to the shed.

Gos was huddled over the empty meat dish. She flapped and started to hop across the plank floor. Warren waited firmly. The hawk calmed and slowly Warren approached her. From his pocket he took a soft jess and tied it around her left leg. Once more he pinioned her wings and placed her on a perch, a young poplar trunk nailed to the shed corners. He fastened the jess to a leash in turn fastened to the poplar. The hawk nestled her clenched right foot into her body.

Warren sat, his back to the wall, and watched his bird, roosted now atop the swivel of her leash. A faint tapping at the door distracted him.

"Warren . . . Warren," said Gretel hoarsely. She had been crying. "Warren, I lied. I didn't sleep with Anthony."

Warren did not answer.

"I swear I didn't . . . I lied. I just felt sorry for him."

"How did you know that detail about his navel?" asked skeptical Warren.

"He took off his shirt in the garden. Warren, don't be silly. I lied. Christ, he's only *twelve* years old."

"Are you still pregnant?"

"You know I am, Warren."

"Do I?"

"You should."

Warren tiptoed past the august eyes of the hawk to the door. He opened it a crack to Gretel's red-puffed face. "Come to bed now, Warren."

"Why did you say those things to begin with?"

Gretel shrugged benignly and sniffled.

"Well?"

"I don't know."

"I have to stay with the hawk," said Warren.

"All night?"

"She's sick and frightened."

"So am I."

Warren opened the door wide, craned out his head, and kissed Gretel lightly on her forehead. Gretel smiled at him. Her lips contorted thinly and she said, " 'Night, you condescending prick." Warren recoiled his head barely in time to avoid being boxed in the slamming door.

He smarted under a welter of vexation, and relief at the narrowness of his escape. She had utterly misread him. That much was clear. It was a kiss of tenderness, of compassion, mused Warren, his nose inches from the pine door. It was a kiss of forgiveness.

The hawk raised her rounded tailshaft and sliced a loose splat of grayness into the corner. Warren rolled his shoulders and sighed. At the least he could accustom his hawk to his presence, the odor of his flesh and hair, his green billiard-cloth shirt and mutilated green flannel trousers.

In order to tame her Warren intended to keep watch and prevent the bird from sleeping. Simultaneously the hawk observed the man. Her black pupils swiftly contracted and expanded as if some arcane code were being transmitted.

The vigil of the hawk continued through the night. She scrutinized the shadowy creature doubled up below her, its head on its knees, a garland of cobwebs festooned to the wall above its head.

꧂ Sunrise slanted incarnadine light through the doweled window and Warren's eyelids. He blinked and looked at the cinder-and-salmon-colored striations across the plank floor. Instantly, to establish his bearings, he replayed Gretel's ruse, the jarring door-slam, his ailing hawk. The hawk! She was not on her perch.

In the dark opposite corner of the shed the hawk floundered on her belly, entangled in the leash. Her eyes were fastened on Warren. He pushed himself to his feet and replaced the mute goshawk on her perch. She tilted, gained her equilibrium, and clutched the poplar with both her feet. Her breastbone bulged from under her brindled ivory breast.

Warren left the hawkhouse and with resolution strode up to the attic. He filled his trouser pockets with ammunition, looped the leather strap of his field glasses around his neck, and grabbed his rifle.

He met alluringly disheveled Gretel downstairs. She wrapped her quilted yellow bathrobe close about her and froze. Warren swept gingerly past her apprehensive face, the barrel of his .22 depressed.

From the granite doorstep he scanned the fields behind his house, first with his naked eye, next through his field glasses. He unbolted his rifle and fed it one lead and copper cartridge. He prowled around the garden in the dewy grass. Again he raised the glasses to his eyes. Shrewdly adjusting the dial, he transformed a nebulous kaleidoscope of colored mist into the more mundane knoll of pine saplings. He focused on a flock of starlings strolling through the grass like violet-green mechanical toys. He raised the cold stock to his cheek in rehearsal. He shuddered and stealthily crossed to the ravine.

Warren had never shot a gun. He had killed a bird once, a goldfinch, in the chrome grill of his car. The wind had meshed its pale feathers into the studding and he was forced some days later to extract the rigid bird parts piecemeal.

He paused behind the dead elm. From his lowly vantage the starlings were not visible. He crept slowly up the knollside. The unwitting colony of starlings came into view. Warren aped the prone posture he had seen the sniper assume on Technicolor mesa tops. He isolated one bird and aligned its breast with the sight of the barrel. The starling dunked under a pine bough.

Warren pressed the trigger gradually and gradually squinted his eyes shut. His mind heard the explosion it expected and he leapt to his feet to locate his quarry. The air filled with a flurry of fleeing black triangles. He scoured the ground beneath the sapling but found no trace of violence. He unbolted his rifle. The cartridge popped into the air. Warren clenched his teeth: he had overlooked the safety.

From that point, birds uncannily disappeared at Warren's approach. Stalking fowl in suffocating spring growth was a tedious affair. The sun glared. His field glasses became a millstone. He unbuttoned his billiard-cloth shirt and circled back toward the road. Warren remembered he had not eaten supper the night before. He shifted his gun from hand to hand and trudged along the ridge above the roadside.

A pulp truck labored up a short incline. Warren waved to the driver. The obtuse trucker in turn beeped his horn twice and shot Warren with the improvised gun of his index finger and thumb. Chagrined, Warren plopped down under a wild apple tree. Brown wisps of petals were strewn around its trunk. He mopped his nape and brow and stretched out, his fingers locked behind his head.

A foolhardy twitter commenced above his head.

Oh, unlucky descendant of the fabulous Bird that capered so guilelessly upon the menacing snout of the Serpent—a sparrow had lit on a branch above Warren's head. Cunningly, smoothly, Warren groped for his .22 and pulled it to him.

The sparrow scolded.

Warren fired.

The bird dropped by Warren's ear and scooted unevenly into thick grass. Warren crawled in pursuit. He parted the grass and clubbed the wounded sparrow to death with the stock of his gun. He inserted the hot limp-necked bird into his shirt pocket.

Swallowing his quickening secretion of saliva, he traipsed down the embankment to the road, the rifle resting in the crook of his arm.

The bird was grotesquely small.

Warren estimated his expedition had covered four to six miles. He trekked along the pebbled shoulder of the road, then, to gain better prospect of his location, tugged a jutting root, and hoisted himself up the incline. Less than one hundred and fifty yards away sat his clapboard farmhouse. Through his field glasses Warren discerned Gretel, squat on her haunches, shaping mounds of earth around the corn kernels that sprinkled from shirtless Anthony's palm. Above the waist of his dungarees a long pink scar smiled from his tanned flesh.

To frighten them, Warren approached quietly, his rifle raised. Gretel spotted him first. She screamed warning. Crouched low, Anthony tunneled through the shaking grass to the ravine.

Warren walked up to the garden, shaking his head in amazement. "And what was that all about? You didn't actually think—" he grinned.

"I have no idea what's in your head, so—"

"So you sounded alarm." Warren laughed gleefully and by the tailfeathers plucked the battered prey from his pocket. "This hunter is after bigger game." Mockingly he jiggled the birdlet before her nose.

"Is this your idea of a game?" Gretel said scornfully.

"Certainly," said Warren. "You see to your Kestrel, me to my Gos."

His hawk was sitting alertly where he had left her. Warren slipped on his doeskin gauntlet and shook the sparrow a step below the perch. The hawk examined the tiny meal and bobbed reluctantly; then she pounced down on his fist, lowered her head and began to tear.

4

First page center of a garnet-colored vinyl notebook, Warren block-printed H A W K I N G   D I A R Y on a sky-blue line. The twenty-third of June he penned his initial turgid entry:

> I have nursed Gos diligently. I have roved hill-tops, foraged the ravines, tramped thicket and field to provide her three small daily meals.
>
> To date, her diet consists chiefly of sparrow, chickadee, and starling. She convalesces rapidly. Pleasant mornings I weather her for an hour in the yard on a metal perch.
>
> Still, small reminders of her truculent captivity persist: a black scab on the top of her head and a brown ring around her right arm (much like a burn).
>
> When I enter the hawkhouse, she flaps excitedly. There is more to manning a hawk than the calculated equipoise of food and the lack of it!

JUNE 24—

> Despite the scorching day I wore my customary outfit so as not to unsettle Gos. At noon I shot the raven in the elm. This was overdue. For too long it had harassed me with its Hallowe'en poses. The gardeners, I think, were taken aback at my marksmanship. Good. I put them on edge.
>
> I fed Gos half a cropful of the raven's greasy breast meat. She is slicing with increasing vigor.
>
> Late this afternoon I promenaded her around the fields for a full hour or more. She adjusted to the rhythm of my gait at once. She was enjoying this stroll when a road grader scraped by. She became flustered. Promptly, I headed her

home. I was unprepared for the pinpricking sensation a glance at the ground elicited: my shadow stretched in the grass before me, the cruel profile of Gos on my fist.

Later this evening I will dismember a wing of the raven and attach its nub to the clothesline for a lure. It occurs to me as the days pass that this household has become severely polarized into two ancient camps: Farmers and Hunters.

JUNE 26— Gos jumped the entire length of her leash for the head of the chickadee garnishing my glove thumb.

Constant arduous work is toughening my body. I begin to comprehend why the true hunter has long observed rules of abstinence. Without a spartan continence is this rate of advancement, this one-mindedness, possible?

JUNE 29— I jessed Gos's right leg yesterday. This morning I fastened a bell above each of her jesses. The bells seemed to annoy her. She pecked at them and ate little.

Once daily I feed her a moderately full crop. A hard rain cooled the air this morning but the afternoon was muggy. I kept her inside.

I extended the length of her leash and she will readily (at the trill of the police whistle or the call of her name) leap the distance across the hawkhouse to my fist. Sometimes I reward her with a strand of meat. The hand of my gauntlet is crusted with gore.

Under my attic window now the ping-ping of the shuttlecock is most distracting. Gretel is teaching the basilisk the game of badminton. This is yet another exhibition on her part—she will do anything to convince me she is happy. I know better. She contrives an ebullient girlishness. She wears beige shorts.

Still, I am insufficiently neutralized.

JULY 5—

Today a clouded milestone! Tonight an auspicious crescent moon; yet it is painful to write.

I tied a fifty-foot length of clothesline to the leash and launched Gos to the lowest branch of the elm. She hunched there and gazed about. Like a scarecrow, I extended my gloved arm, called her name, and blew my whistle. She darted obediently to my outstretched arm. The single unpleasant aspect of this episode was that she miscalculated upon landing and punctured my unsheathed upper arm.

I put Gos back in the hawkhouse and rewarded her with a titbit. Gretel interrupted her bucket brigade to the garden to attend my lacerations.

My green shirt, emblazoned with eight rents, forms an admirable ensemble now with my trousers.

Slyly, to taunt me, the pinging recommences beneath my window. I will repeat Landseer's dictum—Training, correcting, consulting his bird shall be his *main* pleasure.

Damn them. If one of them overshoots, if that shuttlecock is stroked through this window, so help me I will fall upon it like a tiger on a canary and yank out every feather.

JULY 11—

For the fifth day running the weather is unbearably hot. I cannot raise my right arm above my head. Today, after swinging left-handed the meat-jeweled raven's wing lariat-style above my head, I let it drop in the grass. Leashed Gos swooped low from the branch and fell at mark on the wing.

Now she has been tested and proven to whistle, to lure, to voice.

A robin I shot from the telephone wire was greedily and beautifully devoured. Gos pecked away the skullcap of this robin, dipped her horned curve into its brainstuff, leaving a red wick of spinal column; this she tugged with

such ferocity the headless robin turned inside-
out—bursting into a crimson tulip.

Afterward she stropped her beak merrily on my
thumb.

The test is not far off.

JULY 13— This kind of commitment, of discipline, is doing its work. I am hardly tempted now when I
spy them from the window. Gretel and protégé
resemble lotus-eaters, inhabitants of Cockaigne.
They pull weeds, they water their minuscule
plot; then, pretending the harvest is over, they
wallow in the grass and bask—legs wedged
open, codpiece awry, slumbrous, besotted. The
roast pig will never present to them the knife
to slice its own succulent flesh as in that
drugged land of Cockaigne.

They are pretenders! They are miserable.

JULY 17— In the ravine I shot a rabbit that was paralyzed
on a stump, sure I would pass by. Later I tied
fishing line to its hind leg and Gretel (hidden
behind a clump of briars) reeled it across the
field. This failed. Either Gos did not see the
rabbit dragged through the tall grass or else she
balked at Gretel's presence.

Whichever, I know Gos is in trim; that she is
properly trained, manned, and prepared for
the great test—free flight.

If the day is clear, tomorrow.

On my way back to the house the young croco-
dile (hot to capitalize on my disabled member)
challenged me to a game of badminton. I ignored him. I ignore them both. Had Gretel not
tried to compete with me she might have been
happy. As it is, her artificial happiness sickens
me. At heart she is miserable. It is too late. I
am beyond pity. When winter comes, when
Gos brings home grouse and woodcock—then

the grasshoppers will come knocking and ob-
sequiously kneel.
And I shall say GO DANCE.

5

Halcyon afternoon. Warren weathered his hawk in the shade of
the house. Under the baking sun Gretel sprayed the garden
(leafy and pointed shoots already sprouting between stakes) with
extensions of newly purchased hose. Athwart the glacial boulder,
Anthony catnapped on his stomach, his cheek resting on the
backs of his hands.

At two o'clock Warren returned Gos to the inside perch. To
insure a reciprocal keenness, neither austringer nor hawk had yet
eaten. Warren's cumbersome right arm was swollen from shoulder to wrist. Dully, leadenly, it hung by his side as he rechecked
his apparatus.

He employed Gretel's cast-off leather pocketbook for his hawking pouch. Into it he stuffed the compactly wound raven-wing
lure, an extra set of jesses, and his official police whistle—brilliant
metal encasing a hardwood ball.

Gos shifted and began to rearrange plumage on her back.
With his curled index finger Warren stroked her rolling dark-
capped head. "Cobra," smiled Warren, "cobra de capello." Her
flashing orange irides sent waves of nervous anticipation over him.

He slung his field glasses over his neck and carried his rifle into
the bright field. The garden was abandoned. A rake lay in an
aisle teeth up. Warren unbuttoned his billiard-cloth shirt and
tied it around his waist. He crossed the field, rested against the
leafless elm, and listened: the static of mosquitoes.

He scaled the hill of saplings and collapsed grunting in a heap.
A cold unnatural drop of sweat hung from his nosetip; droplets

glided down his sides to the beltline of his tattered flannel trousers. He cowled his head from the sun with his shirt and lurched downhill to a dense stand of firs. A chipmunk chided him curtly and vanished into the thick-laced underbranches of a fir. Warren strayed through the stand. A branch swatted his nose and he tumbled down a steep embankment to the river.

The water was badly polluted. A citron-yellow head of foam had collected before a half-submerged decaying trunk. Warren dunked his head and slapped water on his neck and chest. His eyes burned. A jay rowdily flitted overhead before he could swing his .22.

He chose each step along the bank, noiselessly. Cedar and poplar lined the banks and shaded Warren as he made his way to a sharp bend in the river. He sat on a warm stone outside the elbow of the meander and scanned downstream through his field glasses. Trunks dammed the river below, forming a moss-rimmed pool under a birch tree. Warren let his glasses fall to his chest and twisted his knuckles in his stinging sockets.

A crackling, a splash, and through the haze red-eyed Warren beheld a spectral dryad wading in the pool. He was hallucinating, he thought, his arm had gone septic. She floated on her back as white light glinted through the birch leaves and dappled her breasts, naked belly, and loins. A faunlet rudely appeared and gamboled on the mossy bank.

Warren's field glasses dispersed the sylvan sham, focusing lucidly and cruelly on Anthony's navel slash; depressing to his furless contracted and uncircumcised spout. Anthony cannonballed into the pool with a great splash and Gretel frolicked to the bank. Sunny waterdrops stippled her body. She laughed as Anthony stood on his hands in the pool and wiggled his toes.

Crablike the intruder backed into the brush. When he was thirty feet from the water he rose and scrambled feverishly up the incline. He crumpled on the burnt umber floor of the fir needles. "Slut," he muttered, "pathetic slut."

~⧉ The sun was lowering when Warren's .22 yapped like a cap gun and a redheaded woodpecker plummeted to the foot of the maple riddled by its gimlet beak.

In the hawkhouse he secured the woodpecker's breast to the raven-wing lure. He slid the strap of the hawking pouch over his shoulder. Awkwardly, he fitted the gauntlet upside-down on his left hand. He unhooked the leash and wound the jesses around his fingers. Hungry, sharp-set, Gos straddled his ungainly glove and clenched.

Outside she revolved her head, puzzling at the distant moan of a farm dog. Warren halted at the far end of the field, one hundred feet short of the elm. With a thrust of his arm he cast Gos off. She beat her wings swiftly (he heard the whoosh of her fingers pressing down the air) and sailed to the lowest dead limb. There she humped. Her head cocked from side to side.

Warren fidgeted, his eyes fixed on the hawk, as long as he was able. He extended his good arm and gave a blast of his police whistle. The hawk flapped her wings and pruned them close. Her bells jingled lightly. She settled on the limb.

Warren followed with two shrill blasts. Gos did not move.

Warren sat in the grass and waited. Patience. He counted to three thousand. Presently he took the raven-wing lure from his pouch and swung it around his head, shouting "GosGosGos" with each revolution. The weighted lure dropped in the grass. Gos sulked on the limb. In the lavender twilight her silhouette resembled a turkey vulture's.

Warren blew brief strident blasts on the whistle until he felt dizzy. He tramped to the foot of the elm and called up to her. He drummed his palm on the rotting trunk.

With a tinkling and a rustle of wings the shadow of the hawk left the elm and skimmed over the knoll toward the firs, her jesses trailing behind.

Warren snatched the lure and stumbled up the pine knoll. He sickened at the appearance of the enormous saffron balloon bouncing on the horizon—he imagined a snapping sound, the fist of a child gripping a limp balloon string. Perceptibly it rose, diminished, and diluted to an ocher moon.

Warren bleated his whistle with all his breath.

He whipped the lure over his head.

He called the name of his hawk at the top of his voice.

Impulsively he discarded the lure and moon-eyed drifted into the firs, his ears pricked to catch the tinkling of bells above the hissing trees.

THE
PRICE OF
PINE

1

Pine, the rising price of pine, gave Jeshimon Plantation its life. Logs stacked each winter were trundled down ravines into the freshet-swollen Starks River and driven to the sawmill in Starks. Caribou fled north and homesteaders bought up cheap cut-over land, pulled stumps, drank rum, dragged boulders, drank more rum, piled stones, and pastured their sheep, cows, horses, and oxen.

When the pine near the river was depleted, tote roads were cut deeper in, to the stands at the base of the mountains. And when all the big pine was gone, the spruce drives began.

Finally, valuable timber grew so far from the Starks River, in such inaccessible places, that the number of tote teams dwindled, and with them the vitality of Jeshimon Plantation.

Farms were gradually abandoned or worked in poverty and sour, then dull exhaustion. Pastures and orchards yielded to poplar, gray birch, and ash—cover for deer migrating from the south, the bear, rabbit, partridge, and legions of varmints. Jeshimon escaped incorporation into a township so the lumber companies which acquired the wild reaches to its north might enjoy the gentler tax laws of unorganized territory.

The founding families of the Plantation, the Drivers, Beans, Looks, Peeveys, and Nileses, sold the hill land to the lumber companies, whose machines were increasingly able to surmount any obstacle to extract distant stands of hardwood.

The lumber companies, in turn, sold the land to investors and from the cities heterogeneous armies of campers, hunters, rock-hounds, antiquers, skiers, and admirers of foliage purchased ramshackle hill farms for sums which prompted the Jeshimon villagers to scoff, gossip, and finally despise the invaders who had locked them out of their backyards without a shot fired.

Weathered pine and hemlock barns were dismantled for interior decoration. Retired businessmen returned to their looted farms in June, picture windows broken, and departed for the Caribbean in November. Groups of young people arrived and, in groups, farmed in an intense and bookish fashion. The descendants of the founders of Jeshimon Plantation, however, continued to call the hill farms by their old names, the Bean Farm, the Driver Pond House.

One can still decipher the extent of once-cleared land by rusted blades, stone walls, and orchards strangled in the alders, or fix the location of farms by a shallow interlapped stone well, cellar, or granite foundation. Land, to property, to real estate—the process is completed.

The original invasion of two centuries before is commemorated each year in the brochure available at the wooden prison—reshingled and painted barn red with T O U R I S T I N F O R M A-T I O N hung above J A I L 1788—at the entrance of Jeshimon Plantation:

> Come to our plush woodlands and sparkling rivers. Vacation by our lakes and see our bountiful game. Hike picturesque mountain trails through country unchanged since the time of the fierce Bagog Indians and visit the historic monument of Daguet, their fighting priest.

2

They survived because Senuchus (the "Mary" and "Mary Mussoc" of Urian Driver's *Journal of My Life with the Aborigines*), so close to the end of her first pregnancy, persuaded Wassus George, her husband, to forego Vespers and stroll with her along the sandy banks of the Bagog River. No sooner had they left the stockade than Captain Sylvester Hedge, concealed in the forest above their village, heard the voices of the assembled Bagog tribe swell into hymn and fired the shot which started an avalanche of one hundred and eighty-seven Englishmen upon the log chapel in the midst of the settlement, a footrace whose laurels were the coveted and hoary scalp of the zealous Anglophobe and Jesuit missionary Father Odilon Daguet—"by means of insidious accounts of Our Savior's death, he inflames and proceeds to dispatch packs of Bagog Indians to roam the wilderness like wolves intent upon murder and dismemberment of the English," Governor Wharf had charged when the warrant and bounty were posted.

Wassus George and Senuchus also heard the signal shot and the succeeding screams amid the din of musketry. Senuchus could not wrestle Wassus George from the bank where he knelt, closed his eyes, and prayed for the life of his teacher, Father Odilon. At last Senuchus pounded her husband's shoulder and pointed to the red flames which waved in the crackling air above the pinetips and shone like a sun rising out of the black waters of the Bagog. Wassus stumbled beside impassive Senuchus to the edge of the forest. He wept and resumed such an interminable litany for the soul of his Priest and the souls of his Tribe that were it not for the thunderous conflagration, their hiding place would certainly have been found out.

Despite Senuchus' curses, the next morning Wassus George crept to the blasting coals of the village, gathered what he believed to be pieces of Father Odilon Daguet's corpse, and carried them in his bearskin smock to a bluff overlooking the Bagog River. There he buried the smock and, notching two sticks of cedar, planted a crucifix. Tradition has it that before Wassus descended from the bluff, he stood over this rude grave and vowed to forgive the sins of all his enemies and to live a life of peace.

Shortly, Wassus George approached Senuchus, who was eating a picnic of smoked moosemeat, raspberries, and maize pudding. He described to her all he had seen and what he had done. Stunned with grief, Wassus George regarded his pregnant wife as she completed her meal and sparked a fire to smoke on the bark of the red willow. Appalled by her silence, Wassus had begun to repeat the description when he noticed a large bark basket behind her. It was filled with provisions: smoked meat and fish, herbs, additional tobacco, maize, and kernels of scamgar, a wheat to plant the following spring.

Wassus questioned Senuchus. Unmoved, she told him that she must eat, that she despised Daguet, and to the horror of Wassus George, she proudly explained how she had informed the English of the missionary's whereabouts and daily schedule, along with a sketch of the village, in return for knowledge of the time of the raid so she might prepare her departure and escape. Daguet assassinated, she was content.

Like a rabbit wounded in the flank, Wassus George squealed and contorted before her in a paroxysm of despair and pain until, mercifully, he was numbed into a sleep.

Senuchus was gone when he woke. She had traveled hastily, taking no trouble to cover her way. Wassus trailed her northward along the narrowing Bagog, perplexed as to how a woman so near to childbirth and further burdened with a heavy basket of supplies could traverse such a vast and ever-rockier terrain with such speed. He discovered her prints by the rut of a canoe's breastbone leading into the river and for two days pursued Senuchus upstream. At nightfall he reached the confluence of a dozen small streams which spilled down ravines in the mountains before him. Wassus detected the small canoe under a mound of fresh-cut spruce behind a groove of broken and bent reeds. Here, by the origin of the Bagog River, Wassus made camp and rested.

Morning light was sliding over the mountains when Wassus set out and followed the trail of Senuchus into marshes, through a dark basin of cedar into hemlock and sloping yellow hackmatack, climbing steep rocky hills to the hogback which formed a barrier between the country where he had lived his life and the northern land he had never seen.

Wassus shinnied a pine to a high perch in its first branches and in the noon sun traced the white Bagog twining in and out of the familiar timber basin far below. Northward, he scanned the landscape of forest and meadow, saw a distant round pond, a silvery gash in a violet ring of pines, and layer after layer of mountains beyond. Wassus had momentarily forgotten his pursuit when he saw a gray mist spiral above the ring of pines, vanish, and rise again.

It was dark when Wassus George reached Senuchus by the margin of the round pond. She was tranced, propped against a scaly trunk beside a small campfire, with blood on her lips and the infant Ona Mussoc (for so Driver called the beautiful girl), gnawed belly cord tied with vine, alive, couched in warm placenta between Senuchus' drawn-up legs. Wassus cleaned the infant in the pond and washed his dazed wife's thighs, hands, and face. He wrapped the baby in Senuchus' blanket and examined her by the firelight. Senuchus revived and with a fearful scream begged Wassus George not to cast her child into the fire. Bewildered, Wassus declared that their daughter was a miracle he would never harm, and that he would work to forgive Senuchus.

A long while they lived in isolation beside the round pond. Ona was a sickly child. Senuchus ignored Wassus George whenever he beseeched her to journey to Canada in order that Ona Mussoc be baptized. She railed while Wassus prayed before the altar lit with candles made of bayberry and the tallow of venison. Senuchus never ceased in her efforts to turn the blood of Ona Mussoc with herbs and barks, saps, roots, and strange-shaped leaves. She tramped the pondside forest and the meadows to collect spleenwort, the black berries of sarsaparilla, skunk cabbage, horehound, and gold thread. But regardless of the soups and potions Senuchus contrived, Ona remained beyond cure, a vague languid child who kept indoors once the winter and her cough returned. Wassus George loved the thin gray-eyed girl and dreamed of the day Senuchus would understand the nature of her sickness and consent to the baptism.

Ona was a long-limbed young woman the spring when angry Senuchus, pregnant a second time, clubbed the tame dog which had strayed to the pondside. Senuchus considered this dog a harbinger and burned it where it lay. From that moment she lived in watchfulness and terror. She ordered her husband to construct a palisade around their dwelling and warily she roved the surrounding high country, accompanied by Ona, surveying, and infusing her placid daughter with hatred of French and English alike.

Whether weakened by the child she carried or the vigilance she had sustained so long, Senuchus became unnaturally complacent toward the start of winter. She moved less, often sitting quietly combing and binding Ona's coiling hair with beads and shells. Senuchus stopped chiding Wassus George when she sleepily watched him use a similar bead chaplet for his prayers. Wassus observed the change, the mellow resignation which deepened with the snow and the advance of pregnancy. Once more he entreated Senuchus to permit the conversion and blessing of Ona Mussoc, but in answer was only told that Ona needed fresh meat. Wassus molded caribou-hide socks, fashioned thongs for his snowshoes, and one morning departed in the dead cold air to hunt the marshland.

At the onset of a blizzard not two days later, Senuchus gazed across the frozen pond and sighted Wassus George dragging a travois on the crust. Neither moose nor caribou, but the wasted frostbitten body of Urian Driver, one of the English founders of Jeshimon Plantation, was lashed to the travois.

Wassus cut open the mittens and boots of the brown-bearded Driver and saw the bloating dark flesh. Ona Mussoc, who had never before seen another man, drew back and stared with consternation. Wassus stripped the gaunt body and covered it with furs and blankets. All night Wassus forced porringers of hot water, broth, and tea between the burned lips. Wassus was happily astonished when Senuchus moved forward and soaked the discolored feet and hands with warm peat and wrapped them in strips of blanket. At first he had feared his wife might kill the white man.

In the years since the massacre of beloved Daguet and the brothers of his tribe, Wassus had struggled to forgive the treachery of Senuchus, to revive a trust which like the sparks above his ravaged village, had exploded, cooled, and swarmed like bats in the heated night sky. His eyes and the quizzical eyes of Ona watched the fist of Senuchus swab the smoldering brow. Wassus was overcome with joy and a peculiar reverence for the stranger who unknowing had rekindled his love for Senuchus, and aloud he chanted for the life of the bearded Englishman. Ona Mussoc lay on a rush mat and could not comprehend why her mother attended the long shocking body. She fell asleep wondering and was soon awakened by her fever and stuttering cough. Senuchus broke her nightlong silence and commanded Wassus to return to his hunt.

He set out for the marshland immediately. Were it not for the renewal of trust he felt in his pregnant wife, Wassus George would have been tormented by the thought he had so easily dismissed as he stalked a young caribou caught in the cedar swamp, his knife latched to the end of a long pole—that Senuchus, never a convert, had grown alarmed in his absence and fed sickly Ona the roasted liver of the stranger.

Urian Driver recorded this account of his return to consciousness, reception, and ensuing recuperation:

> I started from my delirium and my ears heard a most doleful sound, the sound of a mighty tempest in the sea. I parted my eyes a crack and thought, like Jonah, I had been swallowed by a great fish, for above me arched a backbone from which curved many ribs, the entire cavity being encircled by coruscant crimson flesh. Fervidly I beseeched the Lord to deliver me from this sorrowful estate in a fishes belly. I felt a terrible fire in my hands and feet whereupon I twisted my head and beheld such a

sight as to believe myself *already* dead and, furthermore, thrust into the steaming maw of Hell itself. Veiled in minted vapors but two arms' lengths from where I lay, sat a half-naked maiden unlike any my eyes had seen. A profusion of hair was parted atop her skull and swirled over each bare shoulder to the flushed circlets on her bosom. The pungent grease which coated her face and slender frame lent her a waxen doll-like mien, an aspect not at all dispelled by her clouded insensate gaze. Behind her appeared a corpulent bundled Indian matron with a rounded countenance the color and texture of baked apple. This formidable woman was in the act of smearing a balsamic salve on the throat and chest of the maiden and to my disquietude, she grinned at me as she reined back the stolid beauty's mane and garnished the latter's distending breasts with a multitude of colored beads. Presently, distress in my blazing extremities increased to consume even the scant perception which had allowed me to witness the aforesaid.

Whatever the duration before I once more regained awareness, I found myself in the midst of a most hideous domestic ceremony. The hovel reeked of incense and slaughter. Long strips of meat dangled from the ribs of the hut and the roly matron was bent over a side of some fresh-killed beast, butchering in a sullen methodical way. By the fire in the center of the hovel, the comely maiden, fully appareled in coarse-woven blanket, skived the pelt of the selfsame creature. An incomprehensible, singsonging and lugubrious wail, interspersed I thought with a French phrase or two, erupted behind my head and I rolled to consider a grown Indian man stretched prostrate before a whittled Crucifix hanging above a hewn candlelit altar upon which lay a gray male infant, immobile as if painstakingly carved of stone.

For what seemed days on end I observed the

reverent Savage smoke the darkening infant's corpse like a ham over a chimney of green peltry in the center of the hovel. This gruesome process apparently completed, the distracted Indian wound the infant in softened skins, filled a rucksack with supplies and the tiny mummy, and without a word to either the matron or maiden, with not a glance for myself, he vanished.

The very evening of his departure, beneath the dripping slabs of venison, the woman kneaded and greased the lean torso of the maiden, sometimes with balsam, sometimes a viscous mentholated lard, but always with a queerly provocative smile in my direction. The exercise reoccurred each evening following supper, after which the maiden slept and the Indian woman squatted by the fire and smoked some sort of cheroot.

During the man's long absence, I at first convalesced quickly despite this alien environment. As if her own redemption hung in balance, the stout woman, "Mary" I called her, nursed me with a succession of bitter mashes, puddings, thick soups, and aromatic broths, gradually enlarging my menu to include breads cooked directly upon the fire, hazelnuts, and acorns, a variety of tubers, some of which tasted like our potatoes, others like turnips, and finally, fruity blocks of fat and meat, fish, and I believe fresh caribou.

Generally, Mary fattened my stomach while the enchanting maiden, Ona, pampered my limbs, for in truth they had been so badly damaged that chunks seemed to drop off as the regenerate skin tenderly took its place. Ona saw to my personal needs with a baffling indifference and the infrequency of our discourse, together with the message I could not help but witness each evening, began to torment me mightily.

Then one evening after Ona, coyly ornamented,

had retired beneath a knoll of bearskins, I resolved to put my progress to the test: employ-
ing a staff, I stood briefly before Mary's stare.
Unacquainted with the customs of these exasperating people, I did not know if Mary's
sharp imperative celebrated, mocked, or was altogether unrelated to my effort. It was *not* in
a dream, however, that rising suddenly from the
bearskins, Ona skated to my bedside, raised the
blanket which hung from her waist, and
hooped it over my raised head! Presently I
heard a second muffled command, the humid
cowl lifted, and like a marionette, glazed Ona
withdrew to curl beneath her bedding. Many
hours I wriggled in Hellfire.

The first time since my rescue, I prayed for
strength, guidance, and sanity, for release from
the uncanny witch who smoked a cheroot in
the russet fire glow.

⋑ Disconsolate from his trek over the icy mountains to Canada, Wassus George returned before the spring
freshet. Nowhere had he found a priest to bless his stillborn son
and the preserved remains were again placed on the altar for the
day the frost would rise out of the ground. Little by little, beginning with the few French words they commonly understood,
Wassus and the Englishman learned to converse. Each time he
acquired a new word, Driver proffered it like a gemstone to Ona
who sat weaving and dying baskets in the thawing afternoon sun.
Emerging from a blind like a hunter to reset a decoy, Senuchus
thwarted each initiative of the distracted suitor, deriding his agitation when her husband was gone, stonily occupied if he was
present. The nocturnal ritual in which Driver had lately partici-
pated had abruptly ceased with Wassus George's arrival.

When the ice had melted from all but the center of the lake,
Driver would limp beside Wassus, punch his crutch into the
muddy shore, and watch him net trout from the turbid moun-

tain streams. Driver related how he had left Starks, the colony sprung from the ruin of the Bagog settlement, and explored some fifty miles upstream with seven other men, four women, and two children, with designs to homestead at the mouth of what he called the Starks River; how his party had been unprepared for the early winter; how he had become lost hunting in marshland, the deep wet snow of a vast cedar swamp, the freezing night that brought forgetfulness. Wassus George recognized that his friend was not yet restored, for as night came Driver grew restless and often sat upright in a sound sleep and screamed.

After the rains, wind swept over the drenched earth, and soon Wassus and Urian Driver ascended the rocky meadow slanting to the round pond and buried the tiny corpse. The burial strongly united the two men. Together, it was decided, they would journey over the hogback to search out the homesteaders. Prior to their departure, Driver asked Wassus for the hand of Ona Mussoc. Anxiously Driver observed the gesticulations and charged gabble conducted over the sleeping maiden. Wassus' serene approving countenance was answered by an outburst of mirth and Driver swelled with hope and confidence. Suddenly, Senuchus chattered heatedly, indicated Ona, decisively thumped her own chest, and the majestic composure drained from Wassus George's face. He nodded to Driver and, severely humiliated, stooped out of doors.

Wassus ascribed Driver's relapse to his rejected proposal, their ensuing journey to the site of the makeshift settlement, and foremost, to the grisly scene that awaited them there. Of the thirteen pioneers Driver had left behind, only two skeletal women and a man remained alive in a shanty two hundred feet back from the river. Tall stumps of trees, chopped after the snow had drifted high, stood eerie sentinel around the moldering hut and great stubbled swaths stretched far down the riverbanks. A fetid stack of corpses behind the hut (the survivors had been too weak to bury the dead) had started to liquefy and attract swarms of insects and scavengers. Before the sun had set Wassus dismantled the shanty and constructed a wooden wigwam around the carrion. Frogs belched, owls and wolves hollered and moaned that evening as Wassus ignited the crematorium and, with it, the shrill memory of the night Father Odilon Daguet was murdered.

"The paradigm of Samaritans" . . . "the cures he wrought" . . . "with the zeal of a missionary"—if not recorded in Driver's *Journal* and the diaries of the Widow Hubbard and Benjamin Peevey, the heroic labors Wassus George performed in the weeks and months that followed would seem the concoctions of an inspirational taleteller. Singlehanded he nursed the emaciated survivors back to flesh, mixed potent nervines for Driver, erected shelters, burned stumps to make clearing, cultivated, planted maize and scamgar, fished, hunted game, and taught a thousand ways to cull riches from the wilderness. Settlers from Starks, adventurers, speculators, a surveyor, trappers, and lumbermen invaded with the summer, and Wassus George, become indispensable, began to long for Senuchus and Ona Mussoc.

At last he sent Urian Driver to summon them to the colony he had created. The newcomers had heard menacing stories about savages and in the beginning they were skeptical of Wassus. But when they remarked his pious industry, benign knowledge, and generosity, when they were informed of how he had rescued Driver and the first settlers, Wassus George was treated with a curious deference and dignity. The Widow Hubbard rewarded him with fitted trousers. The men who offered their camaraderie and rum were covertly amused by his abstinence from all liquor and merriment, and privately many regarded him obsessed, a holy fool.

One week, two weeks more passed by, and neither Senuchus, Ona, nor Driver appeared at the Jeshimon Plantation. Driver had told the people of weird Mary and the strangely beautiful Ona, and all awaited their arrival with much speculation and interest.

Ugly thoughts began to worry the mind of Wassus George however, thoughts verified the morning Grieve, a lumberman, returned from cruising the northern woodlands with a string of colored beads taken, he maintained, from the wrist of an Indian's fresh corpse. Old fears revived in the people as the cruiser described the burly woman's body, how her head twisted the wrong way and her fingers were lacerated and broken.

A bold group led by Benjamin Peevey tried to accompany Wassus George as he bolted from Jeshimon for the last time, but they could not keep pace. Alone, Wassus had moved swiftly through the cedar, ascended the narrow ridge, and while the string of beads was still being fingered by a circle of nervous spectators beside the Starks River, Wassus reached the edge of the round pond.

No cooking fire rose from his dwelling. Inside, by the entrance, Driver napped. Curled beside the central beam, stripped and bedraggled, Ona Mussoc seemed blandly to contemplate Wassus rather than greet him. Hide thongs lashed her ankles to the base of the timber. Wassus hurriedly freed Ona and questioned her. She continued to sit as before, stupefied. With much effort Wassus shook torpid Driver to his senses. It looked as if Driver had been attacked by a wolf. The flesh on his forehead, cheeks, and whole clusters of beard were gouged out, and the wounds were barely scabbed. Driver's infected eyes cleared, his mouth went horror-slack, and he jumped from the bed and shrank beneath the altar, unfolding a narrative with such tremulous rapidity that mystified Wassus understood nothing.

At nightfall Benjamin Peevey and several fatigued companions straggled down the meadow to a spiked palisade under large pines by the round pond. Inside the earth, wood, and hide dwelling, huddled beneath a rough wax-veneered altar, peered the terrified gored face of Urian Driver.

The next morning Peevey and another man briefly searched the high meadow, ridge, pondside, and nearby woods, but found neither Wassus, nor Indian maiden, nor trace of a body.

Later that week the cruiser Grieve guided another party to the spot where he had come upon the corpse and there indicated only a rumpled, darkening cluster of fireweed.

Despite the ritualistic markings which disfigured his face

and prompted a cold inquisition from the settlers of Jeshimon Plantation, Urian Driver denied any knowledge of Mary Mussoc's murder. He was shunned. People considered him unlucky and for twenty years he was not seen in the territory. Conjectures as to the fate of Wassus George and Ona Mussoc abounded, facts were weeded out, and the conjectures grew into tales and legends.

Whenever a hailstorm shredded crops before harvest time, a house burned down, a child vanished into swampland, or a falling dead branch impaled a logger, suspicious elders talked of Poison Mary's retribution and Driver's betrayal of her saintly husband.

Perhaps these rumors would have faded or been ridiculed if explorers who ventured into the granite mountains beyond the round pond had not reported an abandoned hut above a flume. More than once, a faraway human figure was sighted darting into the forest edge. A trapper's discovery of the small crucifix bizarrely fashioned from rock maple was widely regarded as a hoax. Hoax or not, the presence of Wassus George had so imbued the landscape, history, and psyche of these settlers that on the first maps the hogback between the Jeshimon Plantation and the round pond was designated *Dead Mary's Ridge*; the pond, *Indian Eye* or, popularly, *Evil Eye Pond*.

3

Jeshimon Plantation was a quiet lumber town and supply post when a robust, well-dressed, middle-aged gentleman with an extravagant beard and hair brushed so all but his nose and pale eyes were concealed, arrived with a fragile wife and rumored wealth. He was identified as Urian Driver and a stir attended his movements. In vain, eyes searched his bushy head for guilt and a brand.

He had made his fortune by the pen, Driver declared, and was a rather celebrated reporter in the large Eastern cities. Not long after this admission, a copy of the scandalous *Journal of My Life with the Aborigines* was obtained through a peddler in Starks and it was scrutinized by a gathering of men before old Peevey's hearth. Peevey began to read aloud and the audience listened with astonishment:

> ". . . and as the wintry days passed, my infernal lust for the haunting Ona mounted, subtly fanned by Mary Mussoc . . . again and again the malignant hag obstructed the sole remedy for the very disease she had insinuated into my bloodstream . . . under the nose of her good and guileless husband, the fiend baited the trap with the most sublime meat while I, starving and nerveworn, could but sniff, ogle, and circle . . ."

Finally the rapt tenacity of the Peevey circle and that of the *Journal's* author was tersely compensated:

> ". . . so I took the musky and mechanical doll at the zenith of that summer ceremony orchestrated by stamping ululant Mary herself . . ."

Though the *Journal* made no mention of the murder of Mary Mussoc, its subsequent furtive circulation renewed indignation toward Driver.

Shock coursed through Jeshimon when Driver purchased a large tract of land encompassing Evil Eye Pond, Dead Mary's Ridge, and adjoining woodland. Many thought Driver shameless, others wondered why a man would buy his own doom. Most people awaited only word of his catastrophe.

Unaccountably, calamity hung fire. Driver's frail wife bore him seven sons and three daughters, all sound stock, and the dire expectations gradually died with the deaths of the people who had waited and wished. On the cant of the meadow, where long before the smoked infant's corpse had been buried, Driver's house was built, frequently enlarged, and surrounded by large apple orchards.

The great pines on the pond margin were felled and hauled by oxen to become masts and spars. Driver's own sons cleared more woodland and outlined the spreading pastures with fieldstones; hemlock barns went up; the daughters were sought and married; and at his end, patriarch and centenarian Urian Driver had outlived every other man who remembered Wassus George in the flesh and, furthermore, was supposed the richest man in Jeshimon Plantation, then steadily bustling if not booming from the rising price of pine.

DOG
IN THE
MANGER

1

All nine greyhounds whimpered as their trainer approached the runs. They danced on their hind legs and clawed at the chainlink fence. Long necks craned to the ground, haunches thrust up, they lashed their tails and stretched away the afternoon nap.

The trainer raised a pin from the door of one compartment. A sleek black greyhound hurtled out the pen, his coat purple in the November sun. The dog bounded ten yards, swerved, and twirled around his master. The trainer clapped his hands: the dog depressed his wedge-shaped head and crouched through the grass, entire body waggling, up to the man's high boots. Indignant at being so quickly curtailed, the dog flicked his hot tongue on the hand fastening a slip leash to his collar and snarled at the pickerel-like brindle bitch who lunged past her opened door. The trainer clicked his tongue, leashed the bitch quickly, and jogged down the dirt road that wound to a stop at his farm.

The seven hounds left behind chorused their frustration.

The trainer jumped the shriveled ferns in the roadside gully and headed on toward the orchard and high meadow. Both greyhounds paused by the rows of bleached cornstalks scraping in the residue of the garden.

A succession of frosts had withered the landscape. From a ledge above the orchard the surrounding maroon and blue hills appeared close, sullenly compact.

Both leashes jerked taut in his fists and the trainer was lurched forward.

Halfway up the meadow a fat woodchuck began to burr. The woodchuck sat on its haunches unperturbed, its black forepaws lax. The greyhounds snorted from the pressure of the collars against their throats. Their front legs pedaled the air.

The trainer slipped the leashes and away the greyhounds sprinted, over the meadow.

The woodchuck hesitated and rolled nonchalantly toward the mouth of its burrow. It was too sluggish, dazed with fat for its hibernation, and the trainer felt a nausea mingle with his excitement. He began to run after his hounds.

The bitch was upon the woodchuck first, clamping its tail as it dove into the burrow and flinging it into the air. The dog seized the neck, the bitch its spine, and they began to shake it. Yoked by the screeching woodchuck, they cantered in circles on the meadow.

The trainer ordered the greyhounds to stop. He cupped his ears to muffle the woodchuck's long shriek. Greedily, the hounds paraded their catch. The woodchuck's chestnut belly had come unseamed and a loop of intestine popped through the masses of stored fat.

The greyhounds did not eat the carcass, but neither would they abandon it. They sprinted after one another, taking turns dragging and tossing it, and playing tug o'war.

The woodchuck had lost its shape and the sky was darkening before the dogs' blood cooled. They dropped the pulp in the grass and frisked happily around the trainer in reunion.

The trainer absently slicked back the whiskers on their greased hot muzzles. It was always a shock to see how a chase transformed them and to share something of it, if only a rapt eclectic distemper. A raccoon, a rabbit, a nerve-frozen doe triggered the blood of a greyhound's eye and discharged tension that unstrung with the crack of the rabbit's neck, the collapse of the doe, her lungs exploded in a cedar swamp. Afterward, smeared and spent, they would slouch back to him, feral creatures reduced to dogs, comprehensible. He knelt to the level of the two slender heads.

Ears tucked back, eyes protuberant, their dry tongues scraped his nose and mouth.

The two hounds led him through the dim meadow to the ledge. Mist rolled off their shoulders: there would be another frost that evening. The light turned on below over the farmhouse porch. Shafts of light from the kitchen, dining room, and upstairs bedrooms sloped to the ground. Despite his distance from the farm, he saw the yellow windows of the kitchen and dining room glint, blotted by his wife setting the table, and the glint stirred his appetite.

He wrapped a leash around each fist and trotted down into the orchard. Abruptly, both greyhounds stiffened. An apple thumped in the dry grass and the branch above it wavered. The trainer stumbled ahead and yanked them to go on, but they balked and gazed across the orchard, ears cocked in the direction opposite the farmhouse. He slapped the leashes on their flanks but they did not move. They howled a prolonged piercing alarm.

The trainer squinted through the black apple branches. He could see nothing but the long row of stakes on which the snow-fences were to be hung. The hair finned along his hounds' spines. They wrenched angrily to the ends of their leashes. He worked to restrain them. Baying and coughing, the two hounds tugged toward the far corner of the orchard. He wrestled them up toward the house. Hauling and hauled, the three staggered directly between the two points, to the road.

A bulky form, an outline darker than the air, hunched one hundred yards down the dirt road.

The trainer whipped the hounds to quiet them. "Hello?" he shouted. His eyes engraved a bear into the outline. The bear was injured, he thought, perhaps drunk from bushels of apples fermented in its gut.

The hounds shrank lower to the ground. From the farm in the distance behind he heard his wife call. The bear slouched forward.

At fifty yards, a man stooped in its place.

"Are you okay?" shouted the trainer. There was no reply.

People seldom walked the dead-end road to his farm and never at night. His hounds lagged shoulder to shoulder as he approached the stranger, halting ten feet from the lowered head.

"Hey, you all right? I didn't know what you were. In fact I thought . . ." The stranger sidled a step closer, raised his head, comically waved his palm beside his ear, and said, "Hi, Jack." As if fingers cinched the trainer's larynx, his voice was stifled.

The trainer stared into the face before him, a caricature of the face he had known. No skull seemed to frame the head or anchor the features. Indolent eyes appeared to float like buoys no longer moored in the brain. Nothing looked symmetrical, nothing solid to the touch. The hounds' jaws clacked as they absorbed the tension which flowed through the leashes and they moodily encircled the trainer's boots.

Again he heard his wife, her voice become strained and insistent above the belligerent cacophony of the kenneled hounds. "I'm speechless," he said, shifting leashes to his left hand and extending his right hand in greeting.

The hunched man lowered his head, glanced at the dogs, and limped around them to the other side of the road. "What's wrong with them?"

"They are very high-strung. Jesus, I thought you were a bear," said the trainer to fill the space between them. Dumbly, as if motion required all his concentration, the stooped man swayed ahead.

"We have a son. He's almost three now."

The man turned into the driveway. His tortoise indifference, his laborious rocking motion, ate away the trainer's disbelief.

"You know, we actually heard last spring that you went out a window."

"Really?" The man dragged his fingers the length of the jeep.

"Yes, last spring we heard you had committed suicide."

He stopped and twisted back his head. After a moment he murmured, "I didn't come to see *you*." The trainer rapidly walked ahead.

A woman stormed onto the porch, and seeing the green glow of the hounds' eyes, stopped short. "Didn't you hear me?" Television voices followed her outside through the ajar door.

"I'll lock up the dogs, I'll be right in." The trainer pulled the hounds around the corner of the house.

The crippled man entered the globe cast by the light and stood on the lowest step. He smiled up at the woman, porch light whitening the part in her coarse black hair. "Who are you?" she said.

The man made a pained noise, scowled, and looked away. His jaw hung and he turned back to her and gawked at her dark wide-set eyes.

"Mark, remember me, I'm Mark Craeger," and his mouth stretched into a long grin. Craeger crouched up the steps and moved around her as if she were not alive but a marvelous inanimate thing he had happened upon and wished to inspect. He touched her hand. He rubbed the fabric of her loose khaki trousers between his fingers.

"These are not your pants," he said.

"We both wear them."

Craeger grimaced theatrically as the trainer opened the door behind her. His stoop intensified. His shoulder brushed the woman's hip as he lumbered past her husband and into the house.

Straightaway Craeger scrutinized the face of the child. He stroked a twine of black hair from the boy's fleshy bright cheek and it sprang back. Transfixed in the highchair by a giraffe dunking its neck between splayed forelegs to reach water, the boy chewed a porkchop bone and continued to ogle the television. The woman watched Craeger hover near her son and quickly brought another plate and silverware to the table. Craeger sat next to the child. His acrid smell saturated the room.

"Joel," said the trainer, "this is Mark."

A herd of wildebeeste smoked across the savanna, an elephant fanned its ears, a parrot squealed, and from nowhere a lion straddled the gouged remains of a zebra.

"Zebra horse," burst Joel, pointing with his chop. Joel's upper lip protruded and he rested his wet chin on the brass buttons of his overalls. Sideways, he regarded Craeger who was bent close to the plate, noisily swallowing the porkchops, beets, and salad placed before him.

"Mark eat porkchops," Joel observed aloud. "Mark eat cucumbers." Craeger contorted his face, stuck out his beet-mauve tongue and wiggled it at Joel. Joel banged his head against the back of the highchair and let out a long ticklish laugh. The vein in his temple distended and his small mouth showed sharp, spaced teeth. "Mark funny man," he announced.

Craeger took the last chop and stuffed it into the side pocket of his navy suit jacket. "Do you like him?" he mumbled. Joel climbed down from his highchair, toddled to the latched door leading to the playroom, and twisted the knob with both hands. Unsuccessful, he slapped his palm against the door.

"Does who like who?" the woman said to the bristled peak of Craeger's head.

"No, Joel," his father said. Joel flushed, fell on his rump, and gaveled on the door.

"*You* the *boy*," said Craeger.

She snorted smilingly and did not reply.

"This is some place, Fran, you must love it here," said Craeger.

"We do," said the trainer.

"Must put a lot of pressure on one another, so far from people. Not to get bored, I mean."

"There's a lot to do," said the trainer.

"Gee, those are some animals you have," said Craeger. "How many do you have anyway?"

"Ten."

"Ten dogs! That must cost a pretty penny. Why so many?"

"I raise them for the track."

"Gives you something to do, I suppose." Craeger bent forward with a warm smile. "Why do you answer all the questions, Jack; is Fran forbidden to talk?" The trainer laughed and as his laughter died, Craeger added, "Is something *wrong* here?"

The trainer slumped back and benignly enlarged his eyes. "What can I say? Fran, have I cut your tongue out?"

Joel's rhythmic hammering ceased the moment his father rose to unhook the door. Joel pulled himself up by his father's leg and turned the knob. Listening behind the door, a greyhound scuttled to its feet, its claws clattering on the bare hardwood as Joel darted into the playroom.

"This is inane," said Frances. She snapped off the television and began to clear the table. Joel returned from his toybox with a miniature dump truck and fire engine and placed them on the table beside Craeger's elbow. Craeger ignored them.

A white bitch stared from the open door. "This is Milka. We're about to breed her. See what happens, Mark, when they're in heat," said the trainer. He pressed his knuckles along her sinuous back. When he reached the base of her spine, the tail switched mechanically to the side.

"This pump truck," said Joel, steering the red fire engine on the edge of the table. "Hydraulic dumper." Craeger pursed his lips, his eye fastened on the bitch.

Twice the white greyhound warily stalked around the table, stirred by Craeger's new scent. Her serpentine body crouched at last, sphinxlike, behind Joel. "Wow, she's something," said Craeger and started to growl louder than the hose noises which Joel whooshed to accompany his fire engine.

"Don't make that sound."

Craeger persisted. Suddenly Craeger batted the fire engine and dump truck at the hound. Milka started before they hit the floor. Her black lips twitched back to unsheath her fangs. Craeger hissed and taunted. The trainer clutched Milka's collar, dragged her to the playroom, and held the door closed.

Joel gathered his vehicles and rushed to clasp his mother's legs. She hoisted him to her breast. Belatedly his face puckered and he wept. Craeger remained seated. He withdrew the pork-chop from his pocket and in a droll passive manner commenced to chew at it.

The trainer felt his hands and feet go cold. "Take Joel upstairs. Latch this door behind you."

Craeger deposited the cleaned bone on the table and as if he would nap, sank into himself.

"There are rules, Mark, human decencies. I don't know what has happened to you and I don't hold myself or Frances responsible for it. Do you understand that? This is our house and if you stay here you'll act like a human being. You won't provoke the dogs, you will not . . . do you understand?"

He saw that Craeger's compliant posture had deflected all his words. For emphasis, that some contact be made, he seized Craeger's wrist. Craeger's parted lips dropped to kiss the back of his hand. His hand retracted. Craeger raised his varnished sulphur-colored eyes and scrolled his upper lip beneath his nosetip.

"What do you want here?" said the trainer. He fixed upon Craeger's white skin, hairs separate on the boneless cheek. He had no more words. Craeger's exorbitant expressions failed to signify any state of being which he recognized. 'Human decencies, human decencies'—uncanny, drained of sense—resounded like a heckler's voice and heat compressed around his eyes.

"He's a great little boy," said Craeger. He wrinkled his nose and averted his head.

The trainer turned wearily and paced through the kitchen to the dark corridor of the shed. The cold burned his wet face. In the kennel below, the ears of the nine hounds crooked to follow his footsteps. The hounds scurried from their stalls down ramps to the runs outside. They fidgeted hungrily, barking, anxious to be let out.

He switched on the floodlights and descended to the kennel. Hardened by the wind, the ground was already crisp beneath his boots. He let out two males. The larger sauntered over the moonlit field and waited for the smaller fawn greyhound to challenge. Nose to the ground, the fawn dog carefully meandered, urinated on the smoking grass, sniffed, all the while closing the space between them.

Swiftly the challenger bolted and left the other champing in pursuit at his flanks. Their sharp-knuckled paws drummed across the field. They shrank in the distance, merged and vanished. A faint drumming continued, grew loud, and neck and neck they pelted toward the trainer, humped, lashed out, humped like giant ferrets. The fawn greyhound rippled past him, a muzzle ahead. His tongue slapped on his lathered cheek, his lemur eyes limpid, emerald in the moonlight. The fawn greyhound, the trainer decided, would sire Milka's litter.

Craeger stood back from the kitchen window, sucked at the milk carton spout, and once more reeled forward to peer into the yard. He hooted contentedly. Under floodlights outside the greyhounds wriggled like snakes around the trainer.

Craeger jeered and tilted back the milk carton.

Frances' voice cautioned Milka. Girded by an air of preoccupation, she slipped into the dining room, hooked the playroom door, and directly strolled to the kitchen. Craeger set the milk carton on the window sill and crossed to the sink. Silently he hunched beside her. He watched her strong fingers scour fork tines and spoon blades. He confronted her quietly with his close huddled presence until she acknowledged him. "Joel takes to me," he said.

"He doesn't see many people," said Frances.

"I think this is a bit extra special, don't you?" Craeger nudged her and with a grunt, stood straight.

"Why do you walk all doubled over if you can stand up?"

Craeger whistled admiration. "Fifty-four bones I broke. I am a cripple. Fifty-four," he blustered. To stress the point, he clownishly resumed a deepened slouch.

"How are you doing? You're not as pretty as you used to be, you know that, Fran?"

"No?"

"And I know why."

"Well, then, tell me," she said archly.

"Because Jack is a *bad* person," he declared.

"Think that," snapped Frances.

Craeger pressed against her hip. His lower lip drooped and he stretched to kiss her blunt jawbone. Frances lightly shoved him and he collapsed at her feet. He smirked, reached up, and patted the buckle of her belt. "You're going all rotten in there. All rotten." Craeger knit his limbs and folded up at her feet like a great-headed fetus spilled from a jar of formaldehyde.

Frances petulantly filled the sink with dishes, made a bed of the playroom couch, and led restive Milka to the isolation pen at the side of the house. "You can sleep in the playroom," she informed Craeger stiffly. He lounged at the table like a drunkard, swished the carton and swallowed, milk drooling down his neck into his collar. "There will be towels on the bed. The bathroom is on the left," Frances concluded and headed upstairs.

"I wouldn't shit in your toilet," he exclaimed.

Craeger rolled the empty milk carton from one corner of the table to the other and waited. When he heard the heavy footsteps on the porch he listed forward on the table and closed his eyes. The trainer softly locked the front door, turned off the porch light, and stepped to the playroom door. His fingers were checked on the doorknob: "It was this time of the year five years ago we first saw Fran," said Craeger. Craeger had not shifted position. His gray lids remained shut.

"I remember," said the trainer, uncertain whether he should go on, stand, or join Craeger at the table.

"On a red horse. She looked so fine." Craeger's words seemed to roll out by themselves. "What a beauty. I loved her, you know that?" Craeger shivered and sat up. He chewed as if his mouth had gone dry. "What's happened to her anyway?"

"What do you mean?"

"Frances is a *bad* person," he pronounced.

The trainer stood arrested. "And why do you say that?"

"You know full well." Craeger's smile assumed a complicity. His lids flagged. "Good night, Jack," he said with a nod of dismissal.

"Good night," the trainer repeated. That he had not refuted the charge in Craeger's smile annoyed him the instant he left the room. He climbed upstairs and paused. He listened to Joel's breathing, crossed the landing, and sat on the foot of the bed to tug off his boots.

"Well?" The shade-blackened room amplified her voice.

He undressed and lay beside her. He reached out and touched the flannel over her hip. "Nightgown?"

"Craeger," replied Frances. "You shouldn't have let him come. My God, he was supposed to be dead, I thought."

"I didn't invite him."

"Make him go," she demanded, "tomorrow. I don't want him around Joel. He stinks."

"How generous."

"Isn't it true? And he's crazy, Jack."

"You have an awful short memory." She did not answer. "Besides, where can he go?"

"That's not our problem," she said. "You can't help him."

"I care about him."

"Why? He hates your guts."

"Oh?"

"He said as much. He said you were a bad person."

In the next room Joel thrashed a bar of the crib and squealed in his sleep. Frances tiptoed to the crib and patted his back until, calmed, Joel hummed briefly and resumed an even sleep.

"He didn't come to see me, you know," the trainer said decisively on her return.

She was silent, thinking for a long while before she said, "Sometimes I wish I didn't even exist until we got married."

"That's nonsense."

She was still awake when her husband twitched and his breathing deepened into sleep. She heard the dogs stir in the kennel and moan dismally for access to Milka's swollen heat.

Past midnight the high-pitched moans changed to a fearful and aggressive summons. She shivered from a doze. She leaned over her husband and wrinkled back the shade. She shook him. "He's leaving, he's leaving," she cried.

In the white moonlight below, Craeger trundled toward the

orchard. He rummaged in the frost-stiff grass at the edge of the garden. Then he lowered his trousers and for some minutes crouched on his white hams. Then, he shambled back to the farmhouse.

2

Impatient that his day begin, Joel clutched the crib bars and rocked the crib.

"Fine thing, to dread going down your own stairs," said Frances. She tucked her trouser leg into the woolen sock and laced her boot.

"I said I'd talk to him. It doesn't have to be brutal," he said.

"It is already. Why did Joel toss all night? And the dogs? Get him out, Jack. That's more important than your sentimental manners."

"Sentimental? He was a close friend, you were in love with him. Is that sentimental?"

"Get him out," she repeated, her voice styptic.

"All right, I said I'll tell him."

She left the room and with Joel slung on her hip reappeared at the door. "Morning, Joel," crowed the trainer. Joel happily whipped his body.

"We'll be outside today," she said and went down.

Untouched, the two towels hung on the back of the couch. The bed had not been slept in. She kneed open the door and saw Craeger's back curved over the table. Eggshells circled a stack of Joel's books, the milk carton, and the pork bone. "Look! Look here, Joel. A panda is snoozing in the bamboos," said Craeger. He flagged the picture at Joel. Joel squirmed and reached to Craeger. "Get down, get down," he insisted.

"Help Mommy make the oatmeal," countered Frances. She humored him into the kitchen and while she prepared breakfast, held him on her side.

When she perched Joel on the counter, however, his lips refused to unseal for the spoon. At last she yielded and sat at the table. Craeger flattened his ear to the table and frowned like a physician discerning an irregular pulse. He proceeded meticulously to cleave the eggshells with his thumbnail. Each time a shell cracked, Joel's mouth gaped with hilarity and Frances deposited a spoonful of oatmeal. She felt blood rise suddenly to the surface of her face: Craeger's decoy was not for Joel—he had tricked her into sharing a domestic travesty, and each time an eggshell was splintered on the table, it was as if he snapped a beetle's shard.

The trainer heard Joel's laughter before he entered the dining room. This day he had not expected to hear laughter and find everyone seated together. "Good morning, Jack," said Craeger lifting his head. "Are you as hungry as I am?" He smirked askance at Frances, who had offered him nothing. She worked Joel's feet into the gum-rubber boots and snapped up his coat. She failed to catch her husband's eye as he ambled to the refrigerator. "There's enough oatmeal for both of you on the stove," she said, grabbed her jacket, and led Joel tripping outdoors.

He put up coffee and dished the thickened oatmeal into two bowls. He placed a bowl at Craeger's littered end of the table. "Been eating an egg?"

"Eggs," said Craeger.

The trainer ate his oatmeal. He watched Craeger's forefingers swab viscous cereal from the bowl.

"Well, what do you have planned, Mark?"

Extravagantly perplexed, Craeger tilted back his head and narrowed his eyes.

"What do you want to do, I mean?"

"Visit."

The trainer noticed the red light glowing on the percolator. "How do you have your coffee?"

"Cream and two teaspoons of honey."

"Honey?" He smiled, shrugged, filled the order, and served

the coffee. He swished hot coffee through his teeth and said in a tight pleased voice, "So, you really think I'm a bad person?"

Craeger concentrated on the trainer's soft eyes.

"I know you said it. How could Fran have known you used the exact same words about her?" The logic braced him and he sat.

"She does know, then?" asked Craeger.

The trainer paused a moment too long, nodded, and Craeger drank coffee and spoke nothing.

"It would be better if you left."

"But I just arrived."

"We both think it would be better."

"Better?"

"We have to breed dogs today. You antagonize the dogs. And last night Joel . . ."

"Joel likes me," interrupted Craeger, "a lot."

"Yes, but last . . ."

"I wanted to be with you and Fran. There are a lot of people I want to see again. I've spent too much time alone in hospital rooms, so much that I forget how to talk. I wanted to visit you first. . . ."

"It's not possible right now."

"And then maybe afterward I'll travel around, maybe go to Peru with somebody, or British Columbia."

"I'll drive you to town this afternoon."

Craeger drew in his neck and settled sulking, contracted in his chair.

"You'll be able to catch a bus." Resolve drove each word out his mouth. His eyes avoided Craeger and he walked outside to the porch. If he remained in the room, discomfort would prime more words and in the end, he would relent.

He ignored the hounds' hallooing and strolled down to the garden. Cusps of frost lingered in the shadows of the house. In the open the day was brilliant and warm. He pulled cornstalks and flung them onto the pile of frost-lurid tomatoes, purple squash, and wizened black peppers. With a stick he chiseled the hard ground and crawled down rows where turnips, beets, and carrots had grown, his fingers rooting the cold broken dirt to harvest whatever Frances had overlooked.

He stopped working and knelt back on his heels. All at once the fact that he had left Craeger alone in the house surged through his body strewing images of a room on fire, a rifle aimed at a greyhound's brisket. Anxiously he scanned the side of the house. His eyes fastened to a darkness shifting upstairs behind his bedroom window.

He sprang up and ran to the house. He charged through the empty dining room, the playroom, and up the stairs.

Gazing into the rectangular mirror which rose behind the opened drawers of the commode, Craeger gritted his teeth as he raked a brush over his stiff cropped hair.

"What are you doing here?" gasped the trainer, pounding into the room.

Craeger replaced the hairbrush on the marble top of the commode and said, "You never showed me your house."

Only after he had noticed Craeger's navy suit jacket pouched on the sheets of his unmade bed did he realize that his own tweed sportcoat was draped around Craeger's body. "Get out of here," he screamed. He bunched Craeger's suit jacket in his fist and halted. Beneath the jacket was an album of photographs taken from a shelf in Joel's bedroom. The album was turned to a page on which Frances crouched in a meadow to forage for blueberries opposite Frances in her gold swimsuit counting periwinkles with naked Joel on a pink granite shore by the ocean.

"Do you need this jacket?" Craeger asked, holding out the wide tweed lapels.

"Get out of here," the trainer said. "Here." He tossed the blue suit jacket to Craeger. The jacket hit his shoulder and fell to the floor. Craeger disregarded it and lurched slowly downstairs. The trainer picked up the jacket and followed. Craeger returned to his end of the table and sat.

"Let's go, Mark, you can catch the bus."

"I don't have any money."

The trainer walked to the kitchen counter and wrote a check

for one hundred dollars. He slapped it on the stack of Joel's picture books beside Craeger. Craeger officiously read the check and folded it in half. He slanted on one buttock to slide the check into his trouser pocket.

"Now let's go. I'll drive you to the station." Craeger refused to move. "Don't make me force you."

Craeger chose a book about steam shovels and leafed through its pages. The trainer wrenched him from the seat by his elbow. Craeger slackened and was dragged out to the porch. "Now get in the jeep."

Craeger squirmed loose and simpered, "No."

"Walk, then," and he threw shut the front door. He spied the suit jacket dumped in a chair seat, rushed it to the door, and slung it on the porch. Craeger stood where he had left him, the suit jacket coiled about his shoes. Once again the trainer closed the door. He listened a moment, locked the door, and with his open palm began to sweep the bone and eggshells over the edge of the table into the empty milk carton.

Outside, Craeger scuffled to the end of the porch and as if he had reached the prow of a dinghy, stopped short to survey the long hazardous swell of field, orchard, and tapering road. Around the corner of the house he glimpsed Milka prowling the margin of her isolation pen. Craeger stretched and crooning, squatted against the clapboard wall, his knees drawn under his chin. He took the check from his trouser pocket and from inside his tweed sportcoat retrieved a small photograph. Frances' head was lowered and her cheeks facetiously bulged as she perused her pregnant belly; her fingers interlocked to measure, to substantiate its impossible girth. Expressionless, Craeger examined the photograph carefully before he inserted it in the creased check and replaced both inside his new sportscoat. He felt the tremor of pacing through the downstairs. The tremor diminished, dogs began to bark, and Craeger watched the road. A truck had stopped far down the road and he saw two tiny figures begin to unroll slat fences and fasten them to the row of stakes.

Joel took him by surprise, roaming from behind the shed. He climbed the porch steps and approached, coyly drawing cider from a brown apple. "Where's Mommy?" Craeger asked.

"What Mark doing?" Joel asked and quickly answered, "Mark sit on porch." Craeger giggled and pointed out the men putting up the band of snowfencing. Delighted, Joel tittered and sucked on the thawing apple. Presently Frances tramped around the shed, fronds of asparagus and milkweed pods bunched in her fist.

"That's a pretty bouquet," remarked Craeger.

"Isn't it lovely?" said Frances. "Is that Jack's coat?"

"No," said Craeger, "he gave it to me. Know what those guys down the road are doing? Quarantine."

Frances smiled, pushed on the locked door, turned the knob, and rapped. "Is he home?"

"I think so," said Craeger.

Frances knocked again. "What?" answered the trainer fiercely. "We're back."

Craeger chortled as the door opened and Joel heaved his apple off the porch. Frances took Joel's arm and pulled him into the dining room. The trainer slammed and locked the door.

"I forgot the watchword," bantered Frances.

He shoved her against the door. Joel scooted to the kitchen chewing his fingers. "It's no joke, he's warped."

Frances sidestepped meekly and placed the palms of asparagus and milkweed pods in an amethyst-colored jar. She centered the arrangement on the table. "What's happened?" She restrained Joel as he streaked toward the playroom and removed his coat.

"I wanted to give him every chance. Malignant is the only word, malignant."

"Did you ask him to go?"

"He made me kick him out." She saw that the edge was gone from his anger.

"Aren't you going a bit overboard?" She opened the cupboard and pushed cans.

"I caught him ransacking our bedroom."

"Are you serious? What was he doing?"

"He'd been into the drawers. The photo album was out. He was using my hairbrush."

"And so you gave him your tweed jacket?"

"He already had it on. I don't want a thing he's touched. I threw the brush in the trash."

Frances locked a soup can in the can opener and ground off its lid. "Then call the county sheriff," she suggested calmly.

"Just keep the door locked. Ignore him. He'll get hungry. How long can he stay? Pretend he isn't there."

"What should I tell Joel?"

"Nothing. It would confuse him. Keep Joel away from him."

"He's gone out of his way to be friendly to Joel."

"It's a trick. Just pretend everything is the same. During Joel's nap we'll breed Milka. We'll use the shed door, that's all. Stay away from the porch."

"It's not reasonable, Jack. If he's out there we can't ignore him."

"You heard what I said."

He selected two short leashes from a peg in the shed. In pairs he exercised six of the greyhounds. The dogs tried to maneuver toward the isolation pen. The brindle bitch who slashed jealously at the dogs, and a large surly red dog, he ran separately. When he attempted to coax the red hound back to the kennel, the dog bucked and pinwheeled but failed to slip his collar. The trainer whipped the leash twice. The red dog glared and cringed into the run.

The fawn greyhound seemed to understand he had been selected for stud. Leashed, he trotted obediently at the trainer's thigh. He brushed the hound's fine yellow coat in the shed and they entered the house.

"I'm not sure Joel's asleep yet. He was all keyed up," said Frances, turning from the sink. She walked to the landing, listened, and returned. "Don't you want something to eat first?"

"No. Get a roll of gauze, I don't know how Milka will take to this."

Frances trailed them to the isolation pen. Milka greeted the fawn dog at the gate with a histrionic assault and darted into a corner. The trainer shut himself and Frances inside the pen, released the dog, and waited.

The hounds stamped formally and frolicked. Frequently they halted and the dog nuzzled the bitch's ear or butted her shoulder and throat. She stood rigidly, switched aside her tail, and he dabbed his tongue over her unfurling heat. The dog mounted. The white bitch yelped, twisting back to gash his tensed neck. He dodged and paraded about her. His eyes bulged from his narrow head. Upright, his tail stirred the air like a sickle.

The trainer took the gauze roll from his wife. "She's too flighty. Hold him." He straddled Milka and wound the gauze around her closed snout. "Now bring him here to me; you steady Milka." He tugged the dog away and his wife held Milka's collar. His wife knelt on one knee and with the other braced the bitch's concave belly. She blinkered Milka's eyes with her elbow while her husband directed the fawn greyhound from behind.

The dog's glistening red nozzle emerged as he reared to clasp Milka's haunches. The trainer bent to guide it into the breach. Muted by the gauze muzzle, the bitch's screams persisted until the sperm jet was lodged, fully dilated, inside her.

"A tie," he said happily. He was sweating. The clonic lunges of the dog's body softened and the bitch relaxed.

Tousled black hair stuck to the bridge of Frances' wet nose. He looked at Frances and began to laugh.

"What modesty," said Frances, "poor Milka." Frances scratched Milka's ear. "Christ, my legs and arms are all cramped."

"Why don't you go back in?" he said. "It could take another half-hour."

"You can manage by yourself?"

"I think so." He switched positions with Frances. He supported drowsy Milka and held the dog's tawny withers to prevent him from rolling off. Frances kissed his brow and groaned to her feet.

"Bravo, bravo," shouted Craeger before she had unpinned the gate to leave the isolation pen. "Do it again. What a show," Craeger racketed from the edge of the porch. His neck was lewdly crooked around the house corner. "Encore, encore, encore."

Frances indicated her disgust and trudged stonily to the shed entrance.

3

Saddled on the arm of the playroom couch Joel peeped noiselessly out the window. Like the white wing of a moth, the back of Craeger's left ear was suspended outside the lower corner of the window. Joel pressed nearer to the glass. The navy suit jacket turbaned the rest of Craeger's head and his body was clenched against the chill.

"Dessert, Joel," Frances called into the playroom.

Milka looped back her neck and haltingly licked her loins. She gobbled the bit of chicken breast the trainer pitched by her snout and resumed the methodical bath. "We'll breed them again tomorrow."

Frances placed three dishes of pudding on the table. "Tapioca," she hollered.

The trainer considered the white bitch sprawled by the front door. "This litter should be something special." Frances nodded and marched into the playroom. Joel hovered by the window and watched her shadow stretch over Craeger's head and fill the cube of light cast from the playroom to the dark porch. She cupped her hand on Joel's shoulder. "Come on, honey, tapioca pudding." He jumped to the blankets covering the couch. "Mark sleeps on the porch," he said.

Frances carried Joel to the dining room and inserted him in the highchair. He dug his teeth into the center of the dish and wiped tapioca on his chin and throat.

"Are you tired?" his father asked him. Joel scooped more pudding and greased the deck of his highchair. The dish was confiscated. "He's overtired, Frances."

"Mark sleeps on the porch," said Joel.

The trainer glared at Frances. "What did I say about that?"

"About what?"

"Mark sleeps on the porch, Mark sleeps on porch," Joel agitated. His incantation worked.

"Not to say a thing to . . ." He completed his meaning with a nod at Joel.

Frances reached over Milka and snapped on the porch light. "What do you think Joel is, a moron?"

"Turn off that light."

"No."

He rose and slapped down the light switch. Milka moved skittishly to the kitchen. "Because you wanted him out *today* I put myself through living hell this morning. I did what you wanted. Don't go back on it."

Frances lifted Joel between them. "And? Is he gone?" she said pointedly. "No, but we slink in and out of the back of the fort. You think that's what I wanted? To play this asinine game?" Joel gabbled loudly. "And don't say I'm upsetting Joel," she added. "He sees him camped on the porch. He feels how unnatural all this is."

The back of his hand flashed up, faltered, and his fingers lightly stung her temple. Redness stippled her throat and ringed her eyes. Joel went silent, vague. "You had better get hold of yourself, Jack," she said blandly. "Go outside. Feed your dogs."

He followed her into the playroom. She picked out the farm puzzle and the circus puzzle and said, "We'll be upstairs." He loitered, resting on the blanketed couch. A wrecker truck, cement mixer, ferris wheel, two wagons, a sprung Jack-in-the-box, Noah's ark, and dozens of plastic barnyard and exotic animals had overflowed the plentitude of Joel's toybox and were stranded on the braided rug. Unnatural? Her adamant hostility toward Craeger, Craeger's uncanny, insolent, obsequious, and idiotically sinister behavior—that was unnatural. And now, after she had prodded him to turn Craeger out, she called it asinine. He glanced out the window behind him and discerned cowled Craeger huddled serenely in the half-light, asleep.

Listlessly, he walked through the downstairs and into the shed. He clustered nine dishes and filled them with dry meal. He left the floodlights off. He watched the woolly blue clouds mass along the hills and conceal the moon.

Blocking the entrance to each run with his body, he slid the feed dishes past the doors. The greyhounds tried to squeeze outside. Milka's season dwindled their appetites.

A thin cap of ice had formed on the water pans. The trainer cracked the ice and refilled the pans. Tonight the hounds were all the same to him and it was a chore to feed them. Bitter wind seared the matted field and forced him to the shed. He decided to renew his offer to drive Craeger to town. Perhaps the chill wind had changed Craeger's mind.

Milka accompanied him to the front door. As if she were readying to break from a trap, the white bitch crouched below the doorknob. He dragged her to the playroom and hooked the door. Then he flicked on the porch light and went out.

Craeger dropped a drumstick into the tiny heap of picked chicken bones on the porch deck and snuggled the patchwork quilt about his neck. He revolved his head, raised his eyes and said pompously, "Yes?"

The trainer noted Craeger's new supplies. He stooped, and one by one gathered the moist bones. "These can injure dogs," he said remotely. He turned and walked to the door.

"Very well," said Craeger, "dispose of them."

The trainer softly closed and locked the door. He switched off the porch light, threw the chicken bones in the waste can, and cleaned his hands at the kitchen sink. His body moved heavily. A nerve mass in the base of his neck had begun to sting and with each step he made through the house, and up the stairs, the smart quickened.

He watched from the door of Joel's bedroom. Frances hushed

him and resumed the lullaby. Her legs were tucked beneath her and one arm rubbed Joel's back through the bars of the crib.

He leaned on the doorjamb and isolated a puzzle piece by her heel, a ballerina in a handstand on a speckled draft horse. Humming the song, Frances got carefully to her feet. She checked Joel and whispered, "I thought he would never fall to sleep. We made those puzzles fifty times." She moved close to the trainer at the head of the stairs. Her broad angular features appeared to him unusually distinct, yet much farther away than he knew she was.

"Are you okay, Jack?" She did not wait for his answer. She passed him quickly and walked downstairs to wash.

"Why did you feed him?" he asked, but she did not hear or did not wish to reply.

He was leaning on the doorjamb, his back to her, when Frances returned and she was frightened. "I'm bushed. Aren't you coming to bed?" she asked, retreating to the bedroom. He held the banister and as if plated with mail, descended.

He sat on the couch. Hanging from brass chains of the playroom chandelier, the blue coronas of four bulbs nettled him. The rhythmic clack of Milka's tread deadened on the braided rug. When he put his face against hers, the ceiling light, her long skull, and his head were momentarily aligned, just so, and he looked through her eye. He saw only a dark-red web of vessels squirm in amber liquid. It was there, in that web, a sight hound lived.

He turned off the four lights and in the dark massaged the base of his skull and let his neck loll over the back of the couch. Silently, Milka bounded onto the couch and nestled into a ring beside him, her sharp muzzle across his lap. Again and again his fingertips traced a line from her damp nostrils to the bone ridge between her warm velvet ears. When he quit she whined and nuzzled his stomach. He drooped his head forward and pushed Milka off the couch. His foot bumped the Jack-in-the-box and it whistled like a bellows as he moved along the wall.

He fed Milka in the shed and whisked her by the mob of

hounds to the isolation pen. On his way back through the downstairs, he put out the remaining lights. He pulled back the blanket and sheet on the couch and, fully dressed, stretched into the makeshift bed his wife had fixed for Craeger.

Like a blizzard, the baying of the confined greyhounds filtered into the house and he straggled in and out of sleep. Before the night had elapsed Joel's murmurings, the dogs' rutting din, the rumble of the furnace in the cellar all blended together and the air seemed to jangle and scream as it circulated through the play-room. He started up in the blackness, uncertain whether his eyes were open or shut, if he imagined the chaos blaring from the kennel. He turned to the window to see if Craeger had left the porch to defecate but could not determine even the outline of the window.

He kicked aside the sibilant Jack-in-the-box, jarred three carni-val notes from the ferris wheel and stumbled his way toward the shed. The tumult of the greyhounds had grown frenzied. He groped about the mortised timbers in the shed to locate the floodlight switch.

The abrupt effulgence of the floodlights dazed him. From the shed steps he squinted, white-blind, to comprehend the pande-monium below.

Two enormous many-colored wings flapped spookily back and forth the block of runs. Fanning the patchwork quilt like plumage of a mating display, Craeger strutted past the fawn and black greyhounds, stamped outside the red hound's door, and gesticulated his quilt. Purple and white jaws clapping the air, spines bristled, the greyhounds lunged at the fence. The red dog thrashed and crazily rammed the chain-link wall.

The trainer seized Craeger's back and hurled him to the ground.

Craeger drew in his head, doubled up, and sheltered himself beneath the quilt. The trainer stabbed his foot into the mute cushion and waited.

Motionless as a garish fungus under the floodlights, Craeger did not respond. "Bait the dogs," screeched the trainer, and his heel once more came down on the quilted mound.

Timorously the quilt began to creep, over the frozen ground. Craeger draped a quilt-corner on his shoulders so he could see and lumbered out of the spotlit ring on all fours.

The trainer kept pace, exactly beside him. Craeger turned the edge of the house and crawled before Milka to reach the raised porch. Breathing quickly, he clambered, onto the porch, and wound himself in the quilt.

The trainer scanned the flat black sky. Little as yet suggested the coming day. He addressed the murky shape on the porch: "It will be light in less than an hour. If you are on my property then, I'm going to call the police and have you arrested."

An amused rasp erupted from Craeger's throat. "Arrest this man, Sheriff," he gruffly imitated. "The charge?" he inquired. "Well, sir, he's Joel's rightful father." His dialogue completed, Craeger forced a yawn, cocked the side of his head to his knee-tops and watched the trainer's silhouette fade by the corner as if it had melted into the clapboard wall.

Milka jostled the fence of the isolation pen. He drifted by her and the row of pent hounds pranced as though the pebble floor seared their footpads. He made no attempt to pacify them.

From the shed cabinet he selected a box of cartridges and took down his rifle. He pulled the cord of the single bulb above the workbench and wiped a rag along the cold barrel.

He carried the rifle and ammunition into the house. He vaguely distinguished Joel's toys on the playroom floor. He side-stepped them and sat on the couch. He removed the lens caps, drew back the bolt of the rifle, and loaded five cartridges. He worked with precision.

He lay the rifle on the disheveled couch and, one level at a time, moved up the flight of stairs. He crossed his bedroom and furrowed back the shade next to the bed. All he could make out were ribbons on the prim collar of her nightgown. Her deep distanced breaths did not convince him she was sleeping, but it made no difference, so far had she and the bed receded from his eyes. He let the shade fall and slid into Joel's room. He did not stop to look into the crib. He parted the curtains of the window opening on the road, raised the shade, and began his vigil.

More than an hour he watched the dark enclosure of sky. Joel chirped and smacked his lips. The first light appeared, to seep up through the bone-colored road and the hoarfrost between rows of apple trees. Still, he lingered at the window and listened for a signal.

A silver-red sunspot filled a niche in the one-dimensional hill line. Like a snake issuing from a black fissure the spot stretched silver-red along the undulating rim of hills until its limbless train encircled the horizon.

Momentarily, the alert sounded, remote, inexorable, from the kennel and he spied Craeger slouching from the porch and down the driveway. He watched the pallid form veer suddenly toward the garden. It was not the form of any person he had known. It was not a person at all. It was the distorted shape of his life that he saw, wile without spine the lies and deception on which the center of his life had rested.

Craeger made a dozen laggard and undecided steps and halted. He stood absolutely stiff. He turned slowly, all the way around, and he looked up at the single shining pane of glass behind which the trainer kept watch.

The trainer hastened down the stairs. He clutched the rifle and stalked through the house to the kennel where greyhounds richocheted off the chain-links.

He swung open the red greyhound's door.

The red dog vaulted from the run and vanished before the trainer was able to discharge the black dog, the fawn dog, and the brindle bitch, one after the other.

He replaced the pin in each door and walked around the corner of the shed.

Beneath an apple tree, halfway between the garden and the snowfcnce, the hounds swarmed over the bulge of Craeger's body.

The trainer sat on the frigid turf.

The greyhounds' pointed heads converged, bobbed, and wagged savagely. They flipped the body on its back and the four snouts plunged to carve. The swarm became clear, stylized, the revolving figurines of a merry-go-round. He steadied the circular reticle of the scope behind a dog's shoulder blade. He was deaf to the report of the rifle as the fawn greyhound twisted into the grass.

Bewildered, the brindle bitch arched her head at gaze and somersaulted when the bullet bore into her chest.

The black hound bolted fearfully toward his trainer. Steaming muzzle, throat, and forelegs were dark silver with blood. Shot, he sagged and flattened on the driveway.

Frances burst screaming out the front door.

The large red greyhound cowered in confusion over Craeger's body and the trainer fired. The dog yelped and hobbled toward the woods. Frances shoved his shoulder and his last shot hit nothing. Her face was deranged. She saw the figure heaped at the edge of the orchard.

"Set, Set," called the man after the red greyhound.

"Good God, no, please . . ."

"Three dogs."

"My God . . . no, no, you didn't, no."

"They jumped the run to get at him." A red slash, the greyhound disappeared into the leafless trees. "The dogs, I killed them."

A squeal broke from the upstairs bedroom. Frances crumpled on the ground. He put down the rifle. He clamped Frances' elbow and jerked her to her feet. "Call the sheriff . . . hurry . . . do you hear, quick, he may still be alive," and he glided over the streaked frost.

RHAPSODY
OF A
HERMIT

A person to catch fire-flies, and try to kindle his household fire with them. It would be symbolical of something.

—Hawthorne, *American Note-books*

1 *My Departure.* "You look like a real mountain man," Dot had said, slapping my gear. And indeed, with hobnail boots, woolen trousers, a mackintosh poncho over the hump of my knapsack, I suppose I *had* assumed a foreboding, two-fisted, and misshapen aspect. "Sure you can find your way up there in this soup?" she asked. The cold, limp mist had slid off the lake and muffled the shore and the Retreat. Though he stood only five or six feet away, Banok's face was not clear.

"Sure," I said.

The storm door of the Retreat banged and Bayla appeared in long flannel pajamas. She hugged my waist, said it was a dreary morning to begin, and promised to bring up my lunch.

Lynn presented me the orange and brown scarf she had recently completed on her miniature loom. I kissed her infant son's head, kissed Lynn on the cheek, kissed my daughter on the mouth, and intending to kiss Dot's cheek, I missed and caught the hinge of her glasses.

To clean the slate, I decided also to say good-bye to my wife: "Ellie? Ellie?" I called softly. Banok stepped forward, embraced me, pulled down my head, and whispered, "You are so close now, so near the mark." Despite the chill mist I felt my eartips grow hot and without another word, started up the tote road behind the Retreat.

Not halfway to High House, I emerged suddenly from the dense mist. Slim second-growth birch, alders, and poplar appeared unusually distinct under the cardboard sky. I pulled the poncho over my sweating body and sat on the trail to rest. I gazed down at the opaque sea of bluish vapors. Rising red in the distance below, the muted sun streaked the vapor sea with pinks and golds.

When again I started my ascent, I heard Dot's epithet, "a real mountain man." I glanced back at the magical sea of mist, at the magical sun, and continuing on my way to High House I could not resist the impression that I was marching up into a parable.

2 *The Retreat.*   First off, I had best declare that Julius Mabee, my father, was a hunter. He had the cedar lodge insulated, wired, a well drilled, and plumbing installed for his comfort during the deer seasons. It had been his custom to leave Boston with me a day before the season opened and travel to his lakeside in central Maine. Dressed in crimson, together with Hambly the guide and caretaker, we climbed (ironically) here, to High House, an abandoned farm at the edge of the orchard. Father was a heavy man who had trouble walking, so he would wait on the farmhouse porch, listen, and watch between the apple trees while Hambly and I combed the woods, hoping to jump a deer and drive it into Father's field of vision. At dusk, when the deer came out to feed on fallen apples, we were silent in tree stands. We dragged a field-dressed kill down the slope and hung it by the throat, to drain from the maple beside the Retreat. Father relished the fresh deer liver, sautéed. With a board, Hambly wedged the hanging deer's hind legs apart for ventilation. Each year before we returned to the city Father spiked any antlers above the door of the Retreat, all in a line.

Is it possible that only two brief weeks ago our new party, hunting such different game, turned down the road ending at Rust Lake, and the Retreat? The potholed entrance and a certain smell of humus in the wind so potently evoked those hunting trips of long ago that when our vehicles stopped and I glimpsed red and brown maple leaves scoot into the mist over the lake, I expected to see the great gray head of Julius Mabee occupying Banok's space behind the steering wheel. "This is it, Edgar's mead hall," announced Ellie, stretching as she got out of the sedan beside our station wagon. Lynn sleepily turned around, smiled at me pleasantly, rolled down the front window of the station wagon, and collared her baby son, Robin, with a blanket. I couldn't see the lake yet, but I heard the water and the preternatural yodel of a loon. Banok twisted to the back seat and nudged my thigh. "We've arrived, Edgar, wake up."

I *was* up. Bayla was asleep, crumpled in the back seat of the sedan; next to her Banok's wife, Dot, squeakily rubbed a circle in the vapor and squinted out the rear window. We were all soggy and blunted by the long drive, sleeping and waking, through the nights.

Banok took a step toward the front door of the Retreat, halted, shrugged, and counted the racks of antlers on the lodge front out loud, to nineteen. I quickly gathered an armful of split birch from the bin behind the Retreat, and Banok, rumpling wads of newspaper between the logs, soon had the main room snapping with a dry warmth.

Everyone was exhausted and there was little conversation. The two wives busied themselves cleaning and reorganizing the rooms. Dot, a ruddy woman of forty with a helmet of salt-and-pepper hair, cut threads of spiderwebbing with a broom blade. Ellie opened the windows and swatted the teeming flies with a newspaper bat. Lynn changed Robin by the heat of the fire and nursed him in the wicker rocker. Half awake, Bayla stomped into the room from outdoors and grumpily demanded a canoe ride. When no one responded, she flicked strands of hair caught in a corner of her scowling mouth, threw back her head and scurried through the kitchen and main room, opening drawers, peeking at quilts mothballed in the wooden chest, finally bounding up the stairs to reclaim her lakeside bedroom.

Banok leaned an elbow on the vermiculate log mantel of the stone fireplace. Nailed to the silvery barnboards above the mantel were two small photographs in black frames. Soiled orange by water, the left picture shows me when I was a teenager. I straddle the shoulders of a buck in snow. The buck's snout, tongue awry, is twisted up toward the camera by the antlers.

"Did you shoot this?" asked Banok.

I nodded.

"Did you like to shoot?"

"No . . . but I liked to hunt."

"Is there so great a difference?"

"Why don't you two get working," interrupted Dot. I knelt to hold her dustpan and Banok returned to the second snapshot, one of my favorites: I sit in the bow of the canoe, beardless then, my features radiant in the glare of the sun. Pudgy Bayla is waving, her black hair braided in pigtails. Ellie wears sunglasses, a cordial smile on her sleek angular face, the sole paddle across her knees.

I emptied the dustpan and with this manicured image of Ellie still in my mind, Banok and I simultaneously regarded a smudged Ellie strain to push aside the sofa. The dozing infant Robin rolled his head from Lynn's elongated nipple and a whitish droplet streaked his jowl. I heard Bayla's footsteps booming in the hallway overhead, the bustle of sweepers downstairs, burning logs shifting and crackling. I watched the vibrating violet eyelids of the baby, and when Banok looked at me, his nose flattening as his smile broadened, I saw that he too was filled with the contentment of a man watching the construction of his new home, a home long planned, and he said carefully, in his surprisingly high-pitched voice, "The Florida idea was the true one. I can feel that now. Only the atmosphere was wrong. I have very positive feelings about the whole venture."

Twice Dot snorted the unattractive coughlike laugh peculiar to her. Bayla romped noisily downstairs and sprawled on the burgundy fainting couch. "Edgar," she said, "would you put the swing up?" Banok squatted beside the baby and Robin squirmed and smacked his lips. Lynn beamed as if Banok were scrutinizing her own belly. I went outside with Bayla to search the shed for the swing.

Moments later Bayla carried the bundle of coiled rope and I hauled the stepladder toward the maple limb. Ellie was posted at the window. Her eyes absently followed me while I mounted the ladder. Though I was too high to see her (maple leaves obscured her head), I would wager that she continued to watch my uneasy legs on that topmost rung, watched them with the same abstracted listening look of the best, most patient hunters.

3 *Swimming.* The remainder of that morning we unloaded supplies from the station wagon and sedan. The trunk and book-filled boxes were stored under the stairway. Luggage was carried up to the bedrooms. It was decided that until my period of isolation began, I would sleep on the fainting couch, Lynn and Robin in the guest room, Bayla and Dot in Bayla's old room, and Ellie and Banok in the master bedroom. Banok handled his photography equipment alone.

The Retreat was beginning to take shape and everyone was hot and dirty when we congregated outside. The mist had burned off and the opposite lakeside appeared, cluttered with tiny cabins. A breeze wrinkled the lake, ripples catching the light and flashing like tinsel. Bayla picked up a flat stone and skipped it over the water. The stone skidded, hopped high in the air, and sank. She lay on the dock and peered at minnows through a gap between planks. Above her Banok took off his clothes, folded them in a stack on the dock, and dove neatly into the water. His dark head surfaced forty feet from shore and he blurted "Marvelous" and "Come on."

"How Laurentian," grumbled Dot on the shore. But already out of her clothes, Bayla followed Banok's lead and smacked into the lake. "It's freezing," she howled, "minnows are bumping my toes."

Lynn giggled and said to me, "Could you hold Robin a minute while I take a quick dip?" Naked Ellie tested the water with a toe and without a splash slid off the edge of the dock. She is a fine athlete. Even Dot eventually waded in. She sprinkled water on her neck and under her arms and gasped to a halt when water covered her pelvis.

I jiggled Robin who had begun to whimper—and was considering the assortment of white and tan buttocks arching out of the water and disappearing—when I heard the clank of a vehicle approach the Retreat. It was Hambly's old black pickup. His coonhound sat erect beside him like a wife, her nose flush to the windshield. As I walked to his truck Hambly maneuvered the stem of his unlit pipe between his gums. "Sure wasn't expectin' you 'til spring," he said, a brown grin opening up his chronically cheerful face. "Couldn't stay away from huntin'?"

"Things didn't go to schedule," I said. I shifted Robin to get a better grip.

"This here bundle ain't yours?" Hambly slicked back the tobacco-lemon whiskers around his lips. I shook my head and was about to explain, but it seemed so complicated, I kept silent.

"Ellie and Bayla here?"

"They're swimming."

"Well, I reconnected up the water and had the power turned back on like you said. Seems we went to a lot of bother closin' down Retreat last month. You expect on stayin' the whole season now?"

"They'll stay here this winter. As soon as things get situated I'm moving up to High House."

"High House! That so? Poachin'?"

"Oh, no," I smiled. "We're not here to hunt. I'm afraid there will be no more of *that* at the Retreat."

Hambly glumly pouched his mouth. "Things're sure changin'."

"I hope so," I said earnestly. Robin began to screech and Banok jogged past us to the lodge door. His clothes were tucked under his arm. His firm tawny and black body was dripping.

"Feller'd best not run around like that once the season commences," Hambly snickered. "Well, holler if you're wantin'."

Ellie huddled in the water by the dock with Bayla and the others until the black truck had gone away. As I returned to the dock Ellie hoisted herself out of the water and hurriedly accepted from Banok a beach towel smelling of mothballs. Her long arms and legs were goosefleshed and the purple of chill rimmed her mouth.

"Not quite like Florida," said Banok, and draped a towel around her back.

"Not yet," shivered Ellie.

"Who was the old man?"

"Hambly," I said.

"He looks after Retreat," chimed Ellie.

"I see he does," Banok said. Ellie took a second towel from Banok and cloaked Bayla. Bayla is taller than her mother, with my larger skeleton. Her body is remarkably mature for her twelve years: muscley breasts point in opposite directions, her hips are chubby, and lately a sparse silky line of pubic hair has sprung up.

"Say, Edgar, do you remember the time Bayla had just learned to walk and was playing with a sailboat with no bathing suit on and old Julie said she either put clothes on or get the hell out? Remember?" It was a story Ellie loved to tell.

"My father was sick," I explained to Banok.

"Sons inherit their father's diseases," remarked Ellie.

"And their virtues," corrected Banok.

I grew depressed. Lynn put Robin up for his nap and I elected to watch him while the others drove into the village six miles away for provisions.

I rested on the fainting couch, but after the morning's activity the silence was unpleasant. Quietly, I went upstairs to check Robin. He was asleep on his back. His mouth was open. I ran my palm over the warm scalloped terrain of his oiled head and he did a sudden silent frog kick and rolled onto his belly. I lay on the mattress beside him, and noting how the guest room already exuded Lynn's provocative yet functional mother-musk, I dozed.

4 *Antlers.* During those days below, I helped caulk and putty windows, put up the storm windows and door, staple tarpaper around the sills of the Retreat, and I made several trips here to stock High House with a month's provisions. I cut and stacked wood on the farmhouse porch and tacked clear plastic over the broken windowpanes.

Evenings at the Retreat naturally became a gathering, talking time. After supper we sat around the oak table and listened to Banok's plans for spring. He is convinced that the genuinely revolutionary tools of the new era are to be hoes, rakes, and wheelbarrows. The symbols Banok attached to garden implements, hunting, food, children, animals' pastures, windows, doors, to our departure from Florida, and especially to my approaching withdrawal, charged all our activities with a new importance and, often, a pressure.

Sometimes Banok even spoke of us all ultimately fused into a *seven-headed prophetic unit.* It was then that Lynn looked up from her miniature loom, her long young face aglow. Other times Banok would ask if one law sufficed for the hare and the greyhound. Inevitably, Dot riddled his monologues with her jibes, singsonging nonsense like "Is there common law for fox and ox, crow and doe?" Banok dealt with all the intrusions of his mordant wife with the same soft pained smile, and continued, shutting his eyes to concentrate. What else could he do?

One evening Banok said nothing at all and the session flagged. He stared at me. Lulls in conversation have always unnerved me. The wine on the table quivered slightly in the glasses.

"Sooner murder an infant in its cradle than nurse unacted desires," quoted Banok, addressing me at last.

"Keep an eye on Robin, honey," Dot advised Lynn. Robin groggily thrust his tongue out, pulled it in, and slouched in the curve of Lynn's belly.

"Unacted desires, the memory of years and years of unacted desires, of congestion," said Banok, lugubrious bars of wrinkle on his high brow.

"You don't really mean murder?" asked Lynn bashfully.

"You must realize that Dot is an extraordinarily *literal* woman," concluded Banok.

The morning before my departure from the Retreat, Banok concealed the fine black notebook I now am using beneath his jacket and accompanied me up the ridge to High House. From the ramshackle porch steps of the tiny farmhouse we could see splotches of the Retreat's cedar-shingled roof through the thinning foliage, and beyond, the long black expanse of Rust Lake. We sat together a moment without speaking.

"I don't know if I can do it," I confessed.

"I know," said Banok, pulling the black book from his stomach and presenting it to me. "Every day I want you to write in this book," he said, rapping on the cloth binding. "You can't stop now. You must go on and meditate and exercise and, most important, write about the confusions of this past year. Write it down. There are many methods to rid oneself of the *Shroud*, Edgar, you have found yours. Write. Memory is the warehouse of the *Shroud*. Extract these memories, pull them out like porcupine quills from a dog's nose. They say that in time quills work their way deep, into a dog's brain, so deep that in the end the dog dies. Fill up these pages, Edgar, and live." Banok squeezed my knee, zipped his jacket, and strolled to an apple tree. He filled his pockets with hard winter apples and headed through the spruces and down the path.

I remained on the steps, my head bowed, my eyes fastened on a random spear of yellowed witchgrass. It was then I had my idea. I leaped up and loped past the long-unpruned apple trees, after Banok.

My idea to remove the nineteen antler racks from the front of the Retreat that very afternoon delighted Banok, who further suggested that he film the entire disposal. Banok had employed this same therapeutic technique—the simulation before his small movie camera of one's disturbing fantasies, recurrent day- or nightmares, and what he called "symbolic actions"—with great success at his seminars at Ponce Beach, Florida. The virulence of these discomforting phenomena is somehow assuaged when the affected can lounge in sympathetic company and leisurely observe a dramatization of his own psychic turmoil. My wish to remove the antlers fell into the category of symbolic intentions.

As it happened, I keenly felt my clumsiness and only with great effort did I manage to keep my footing on the wavering stepladder as I pried off one weather-bleached antler after another with a crowbar. His camera whirring and clacking, Banok was ever in motion, now flat on his back, now leaning against the lodge or climbing two rungs up the ladder.

Bayla stacked the fallen antlers into one thorny mound. "Christ, what a cartoon," judged Ellie harshly, and she withdrew to prepare dinner.

I weighted the stern of the green canoe low into the water, the middle of the canoe was heaped high with bones, and perched in the bow was Banok, his dogged camera on me. The weight lifted from my mind that afternoon far superseded the weight of all those antlers, covered with silt now at the bottom of Rust Lake.

Banok cut short the after-dinner dialogue on the eve of my departure so I should have a long sleep, but hours after they had gone to bed I found myself on the burgundy fainting couch, elevating first my head, then my legs, unable to find a pleasing posture. Finally I went to my knapsack. From under Banok's *The Eye of the Vortex* I took the illustrated volume of William Blake's poetry which Banok had given me and again settled on the couch. Those watercolors of overdeveloped bodies with contorted faces drifting under indigo water, crawling over parched earth, wound in snakes and chains, searing in pointy red and yellow flames, so aggravated my state of mind that I could discover no rationale whatever behind my impending departure from the Retreat. Yet strangely, as my misgivings strengthened, so too did my certainty that in hours I would hike up the tote road to High House. Across my mind flashed a modified picture of Nebuchadnezzar, foolish as a circus lion, clawing the quarter mile to High House with a knapsack strapped to his shaggy back. No more of Blake I decided, and shut the book.

I found some respite in the certainty of my departure. Later I could understand why. At sunrise everyone expected me to leave. The choice was made. I was to stay at High House, scrupulously exercise, let my poison onto these pages. But what if I longed to return? The way I had so wanted to return from summer camp as a child, from college as a youth, from graduate school as a man? What kind of isolation was one quarter mile?

All the abstraction couched in exemplary parable that I had pondered, all the events that made the continuation of my role as husband and father an impossibility, and all Banok's gentle directives were compressed into an idiotically redundant "I'm going and that's that."

I was wide awake musing on the riddle of suntans when Lynn carried Robin downstairs, tapping between his shoulder blades. I was fatigued and my mind was racing in an increasingly absurd fashion. Somehow it seemed unfair that Banok should be able to bask in pointy red and yellow flames and his skin grow richer, darker, and more lovely, while my own was scorched in a mild sun, to blister, itch, and peel.

"I think what you're doing is a wonderful thing," said Lynn drowsily. Her robe parted and she hefted each breast to judge the fuller and inserted a nipple between Robin's groping gums. To be honest, I usually watched Lynn's humble brow or looked askance while she performed this task, but at that moment I unconsciously traced or, better, traced with wonder the cloudy blue vein branching down the side of her swollen breast.

Lynn said, "I mean when Robin gets self-sufficient, I hope he does exactly the same."

5 *High House.* A shell with an orange tin roof is all that remains of my new home. The shed has buckled into the vegetable cellar, which is filled with rotten beams and weeds. The cellar's stony walls form a trough leading to the vestige of barn, a granite-slab rectangle enclosing a snarl of passed raspberries, a disabled wagon, rusted machinery, and burrs. The morning I arrived I tried to keep busy. I blocked off the upstairs with a sheet of plastic. The pantry has evidently housed porcupines. Shelves and edges of the cupboards are smoothly gnawed and lumpy droppings carpet the pantry floor. The stink of the porcupines (a hot nervous sweat-smell) pervades the farmhouse, but I am already growing immune to it.

I furnished my room, the chimney room in the front, with the few objects I found in the rest of the house. Together, my pine bed, woodstove, slant-top desk, stool, and pyramid of new cans and old pots and pans suggest a hermit's cell, the skeletal stage set of some bleak and modern drama. In the center of this spareness I sat on the warped pine-board floor and stretched flat on my back. I closed my eyes, flexed and released my toe muscles, calves, rolled my kneecaps, thighs—I was too exhilarated to concentrate on relaxing exercises. My eyes would travel from the crude yellow-painted rose carved on the headboard of my bed to the cast-iron bugler with distended cheeks profiled on the woodstove door.

With excitement bolstered by weariness, I walked out on the porch. Far from lifting, the pallid murkiness from which I had but lately emerged rolled toward me like a tidal wave. The magical sun had dwindled to a gray slash in the blackening sky. For a while I halved birch sections with single agreeable knocks, but the unsolicited memory of my father sourly driving golf balls into the garage net abruptly dispersed my well-being. I sank the axe into the chopping block and again assumed a supine position on the pine-board floor.

The advancing fog pressed the window as if it would break what panes of glass were left and come in. I studied the uneven calcimined ceiling, but once more I could neither concentrate, properly breathe, nor relax.

I began to brood: this ability to discipline oneself, to withstand the denials of isolation, seemed a matter of complexion, of genetics. And what complexion had I inherited? True, my father fancied himself a loner, but he had scarcely spent a solitary moment in his life. The single time he had ventured to the Retreat alone, his final expedition, he had returned to Boston transformed (rendered childish by a brain disorder that numbed and, shortly, killed him), and to his end radiantly believed he had conversed with a mermaid in the pickerel swamp at the village end of Rust Lake. And Mother had visited the Retreat only when the humidity of the city summer became "unendurable," shortly pronounced herself "woods queer," and flew to the city. To the time of her fatal heart attack Mother threatened to remain in Boston whenever Julius threatened to retire in Maine.

I followed the wallpapered wainscoting around the room. Encased in florid diagonals, a faded man wearing a broadbrimmed hat paddled a punt toward a millhouse and a dog. One diagonal was linked to another, each imprisoning its own paddler in doldrums, and as I wandered into sleep I imagined that somewhere within me a concatenation of chemicals had decreed, "Impossible, you cannot."

My legs were drawn up, the back of my hand poised on my temple, when the rain-beaded hood of Bayla's slicker poked in the door. She eyed me, bemused, unable it seemed to ascertain whether I was asleep or had assumed an unnatural thinking position. She tiptoed into the room and placed a brown bag on the desk.

I smiled heartily and sat up. "I'm sorry," said Bayla, "I'm bothering you. Here are sandwiches."

"Don't be silly," I laughed, and got to my feet. I cleared my throat and moved to the window. "Thank you, Bayla," I said, but then, suspended, I sighted her yellow raincoat weave in the cold drizzle through the orchard and behind the black spruces, eclipsed. I ran onto the porch and called to her, but not loudly enough.

Discouraged, I eventually scooped a handful of wood chips and kindled a fire. I ate an egg-salad sandwich and watched the air darken prematurely. The sweet warble of a cricket sounded from somewhere in the room. I pumped the gas lantern, ignited its droopy filaments, the warble ceased, and I sat in the sibilant blue glare. Though my first day of isolation had not ended, I found myself powerless to combat a melancholy cluster of forced images, images which renewed their ferocity of assault each time I endeavored to resist them: Julius vengefully topping golf balls, the charmingly bridal yellow rose on my headboard, yellow slicker in the drizzle, the porcupine lavatory. I was unprepared. It seemed inevitable that I would be incapable of filling the long hours, of keeping clean; that I was destined to become coated with hair, to become a stinking, pensive, the more stinking for its pensiveness, porcupine.

I carried my stool outside and sat on the porch. The drizzle was letting up and a breeze had begun to clear the evening sky. With an exposion of anxiety, I distinguished a blue thread of smoke waggle into the purple air below. In a cloud of self-despisal, shame, and indulgence, I sauntered across the wet field toward the gateway of spruce, and the descent. A startled rabbit bounced over the slick heavy leaves before my feet. All around droplets fell from the branches.

I slowed, cautiously neared the Retreat, and hid in the birch grove directly behind. I hunched there. Whose shadow it was that flickered behind the window I could not discern, but suddenly the prospect of being discovered, so close, terrorized me.

How acute their disappointment would have been. For me Banok had come to Maine. Ellie would have sneered, Dot smirked, Bayla wept, and Lynn been baffled. I ducked and sidled away from the orange parallelogram of light on the soggy birch leaves. Never again shall I be drawn down to the Retreat —not, at least, until I have filled a respectable portion of this notebook, and some of their expectations.

6 *Alone.* Down below I hear the ropes of the swing bray against the maple limb. A moment ago something dark and small flicked by the window. Damnation! How is one ever to bridle one's senses? It is only natural to posit a swinger, Bayla probably, scuffing her sneakers in two worn spots to slow down. And what sped past my window? A leaf outside the clear plastic, a large bird far away? There has been such an abundance of distraction these past cold nights. In the half-cellar beneath me begins that series of scratches, snorts, and grunts. Raccoons pause at the spring to scrub their paws or they merely case the premises. A toad burrows under leaves, field mice patter behind the wainscoting at the prying volleys of owls. Furthermore, prong-tailed crickets, some of an astonishing size, infest my quarters.

Today, for example—I concentrated on the spot where my eyebrows merge. By dint of supreme exertions I had checked my brigand senses: my eyes were sightless, tongue dormant, nostrils unreceptive; I had nearly attained a blissful state of Non-sense when the dervish of a single housefly expiring on the window sill diverted me back to myself.

One housefly can block the road to all eternity!

So often during my preparations I have wanted confidence, vascillated, but quick as such thoughts Banok would wag away my frets with his tufted index finger, lower his black lashes, and say, "Stop these doubts, I beg you." Perhaps, at long last, my doubts have ceased. I feel no qualms over having transferred the burden of my family position onto Banok's shoulders. Banok patiently mans the home craft. He shelters Ellie. He has

become a virtual father to Bayla, while I ready to explore the
unknown, to footprint a virgin planet.

THE MOST SUBLIME ACT IS TO SET
ANOTHER BEFORE YOU

And if my doubts have not totally ceased, things are nonetheless
much improved. The Retreat magnetizes me no more than a
picture postcard. At daybreak a flocculent mist cushioned the
Retreat and it appeared obscure, serene, angelic even. Last
night, despite the many and alluring configurations its chimney
smoke assumed, I easily retained mindfulness. Like the whole
of this mercurial material world, the Retreat is the shifting
creation of cloud patternings, foliage, twilight, in a word, Perception. Or there are numerous Retreats. Or none at all! I
ramble, but recollecting this past year, I seem equally elusive,
amorphous; just so reliant upon conditions.

Mercifully, I am a changed man.

Certainly my appetite has altered, my needs have diminished.
Once I was a great meat-eater (every suppertime chops or a
steak) yet for breakfast I ate a snack-packet of dry cornflakes and
drank a glass of cold spring water and I have just finished the
stale last half of the last egg-salad sandwich Bayla delivered.

We might have chatted had she not been leery of interrupting
the flow of my work. But was it consideration? Or is she afraid
of her own father? Do I bore her? Shyness? Bayla is a quirky
child. She seldom sees a playmate. I have been a distant father,
I suppose, absorbed in my work. Also, Ellie has always lacked
maternal warmth. And in addition, one must consider the hec-
tic, strained atmosphere of those ugly knotted months we spent
last year at St. Hubert's Preparatory School for Boys. Ellie was
thirty-three; Bayla a fetching girl of eleven; my precursor, my
former self, was a despot, and thirty-two.

Less than one hundred miles from High House, St. Hubert's
sits in a hollow of the Screw Auger Hills. One must approach
the school cautiously at the start of autumn. Bedazzled by the
opulence of the roadside trees, the unwary motorist is disarmed
when a clever hidden turn reveals the fluted pillars of Hamlin

Gymnasium and he is hopelessly captivated by squadrons of cross-country runners prancing about in emerald shorts. In this manner was I beguiled, as by a spell, to wake and find myself co-proctor of Hamlin Dormitory, director of the school theater, and coach of the junior varsity soccer team.

Why was I vulnerable to this lightning seduction? Why was Ellie similarly charmed? Simply, our resistance was gone. The abandonment of my doctoral thesis, *The Prophetic Writer in English/American Literature,* had left us frayed, deflated. Regardless how ingeniously I had assembled the puzzling fragments of my research, the vital link, the one bright-colored chip that would have unified and illuminated the entire mosaic, eluded me.

Quiet, apart, St. Hubert's seemed an oasis tucked in the granite hills. Ellie may have considered it merely a respite from the rigors of my scholastic quest, but for me St. Hubert's was a lantern dissolving the mist, a way out.

All was not well with us. Again the whereabouts of one vital link, this time the energizer of my marriage, mystified me. From my present vantage this link is laceratingly clear—Ellie's confidence in me had atrophied.

And perhaps justly.

Earlier in our marriage I was her seeing-eye dog. She came to me feelingly and she was trustful. Her dependence gave me buoyancy and strength. I described the world to her.

After an evening of chatter with new-found acquaintances I would interpret for her what was *really* said, the subtle conversational ruses, those gestures not readily apparent. What can make a man love more, more trust in his vision than a wife's acquiescence to that vision? Ellie's countenance, lustrous with the knowledge I would never deceive her, cried, "I don't know what to think. I miss everything. I don't know what has been lost or won until you talk to me." I was her perception, and we were contented.

I had attained this stature quite literally because of my weak stomach. Over the years (along with those mandatory childhood misadventures) she had catalogued her previous love affairs. I listened with compassion, but without fail, any particular of a former lover, his alligator belt or a black wen behind the lobe of his ear, caused me to vomit.

Ellie was flattered.

The purity of violence triggered by her sordid recollections gave her eloquent testimony of my sensibility and my love. Ellie was enamored by my unique combination of a forgiving mind and a concerned if stern and didactic stomach. And I knew she was.

The summer day arrived, however, when Ellie received a letter from one of the shadowy males inhabiting her past. To my surprise, when confronted by this paper touched by a man who had touched my wife, while I fingered the envelope his tongue had wetted—I had imagined the arrival of such a letter a thousand times and a thousand times I had brutalized the hazy correspondent—I was at a loss to muster an appropriate emotion. The letter, written in a flat hackneyed style, was genial enough and made no demands. I did notice Ellie's trepidation as she surrendered the letter, and it nettled me. I asked if the letter meant anything to her. She said that was up to me.

Before I could summon a reply I was kneeling on the bathroom tiles, my face over the hopper, my forefinger wedged to its hilt down my throat. Outside I heard Ellie's groans through my rhythmic heaves.

A sudden unnatural laughter rattled at the bathroom door. I was appalled. Never shall I forget her twisted red face, eyes meanly ablaze. I pulled my forefinger from my mouth, flushed the toilet, and broke into sobs.

Ellie turned her back on me. I rose and followed her. "All the other times were genuine," I said, "this is the only time I've tampered. Forgive." Ellie shook her head, unable to look me in the eye.

"Then I will kill myself," I said, and strode to the mantle where a shotgun then rested on pegs. I loaded it with two snubby slugs and turned a last time to my wife. "Well?" The choice was hers.

As if unbearably fatigued, she trod upstairs and softly shut our bedroom door.

The deeper I ventured into the forest, the blacker my spirits became. I sat on a lichen-crusted boulder for fifteen minutes before I shot a slug into the air and waited for her footsteps. I knew Ellie might figure me to feign suicide, to reverse our positions by utilizing her sympathy. At the discharge of the second slug, however, she would not be so sure. Hysteria would not be long in coming, and I planned to leap down from that boulder, as from heaven, and kiss her. I shot the second slug and listened to its echo carom off the hills. I waited, but heard nothing. I saw only a fox squirrel with his hands together, bowing. I waited until dark before I returned to the Retreat.

Bayla was in the dirt playing jacks. Ellie stood at the laminated sideboard, morosely shredding a head of lettuce. She did not turn around when I entered.

"Roquefort or garlic dressing, Lazarus?" These were her exact words.

For that single deception on the bathroom tiles, all my former honest indignation tempered by compassion she rendered counterfeit and I was forever cast a farcical tyrant, wielding my forefinger as one might a scepter.

7 *Ronald Krebler and Dash.* Following the appointment at St. Hubert's, the disintegration of my marriage was checked by two factors: understandably, we were united by a concern for our daughter's adjustment to that community of two hundred growing young men; but unforeseen (and paradoxically, what promised to mend my ruptured union) were the bald flirtations made Ellie by Ronald Krebler.

Our concern for Bayla was temporarily mollified by her instant friendship with Gwendolyn, the insouciant thirteen-year-old daughter of Headmaster Dwyer. While Bayla attended special tutorials for under-aged faculty children, Ellie initiated an extracurricular crafts club. Ellie quickly regained some of her energy and brightness. She even agreed to design costumes and make up the cast for the year's major production, an all-male *Saint Joan*. I ingenuously attributed her new-found vivacity to our impending conciliation.

As for Krebler, he was another matter. My first encounter with him should have alerted me. The day of our arrival I was showering in our ground-floor flat in Hamlin Dormitory when the water turned so hot my neck and armpit were scalded. I was incensed. Ellie knew I could not tolerate an abrupt fluctuation in water temperature yet defiantly, the cold tap in the kitchen had been turned. I leapt from the shower stall and with tightened fist made my way to the kitchen.

Beside the refrigerator Ellie scooched to stroke an emaciated eight-inch dog. The dog was lapping water from one of our cereal bowls. A blade-headed man with a blond mustache smilingly bowed and said, "Ronald Krebler, your co-proctor. I teach English. And this is Dash my Italian greyhound. Another time."

He snapped his fingers, the dog sprang into his arms, and he left. Ellie leaned against the sink and laughed. She threw me a dish towel. "Loincloth," she grunted. Defiled, I hung fire until she added, "Meet Dash, the Italian greyhound. A perfect miniature of Master Krebler."

In the faculty lounge the evening of the shower incident I detected that my presence elicited an almost chemical rejection from Krebler, whereas my absence coupled with Ellie's presence inevitably attracted him to her side. I would go to one side of the lounge to pour tea and return to glimpse Krebler's tweed leg exit from the door nearest Ellie's armchair. I shared my hypothesis with my wife.

Krebler soon joined the crafts club and, according to Ellie, constructed "atrocious mobiles" he promised to suspend from the attic ceiling of his quarters in Hamlin Dormitory. Once, on seeing Krebler lead his veiny dog toward the dormitory, I conspired with Ellie in an experiment: I left for a brief stroll, nodded to

Krebler, and in support of my hypothesis later discovered him with Ellie, listening to music in my living room. Immediately, after the most perfunctory civilities, he and Dash departed.

But my insight was most blatantly demonstrated on Sunday afternoon when the gymnasium pool was reserved for faculty. Weekly after a dip I would shower, dress, and take position in the spectator ramps high above the pool. And each week, like a squid, Krebler would glide under the turquoise water to the spot where Ellie dangled her feet, hoist himself onto the tiled poolside and grossly display the knob in his scarlet tank suit.

Until the start of the spring semester this seesaw provided Ellie and me a source of amusement and even affection. To jest about the crude wiles of this meager parody of an adulterer—enough.

I was a man in a trance. Why, if only I had not gloated. If directly I had admonished Krebler rather than play him, the fever might have broken. The pain been averted. All so clean and simple. Filliped like a fly from my shoulder . . .

> I was angry with my foe
> I told it not, my wrath did grow.

8 *Dramatics, I.* Unwisely, it seems, I shunned the post-meal intrigues of the faculty lounge and devoted myself to forging a troupe of actors. While Ronald Krebler scrimmaged his varsity soccer squad, earnestly tooted his whistle and sprinted downfield to direct the execution of their intricate maneuvers, I allowed my less ambitious players to cavort on the subordinate playing field. My interest of course was not soccer, but the expressions of the moving body. Which boy tended goal with the assurance and grace of a potential Maid of Lorraine, who booted with the swagger of Gilles de Rais, dribbled with the Dauphin's feeble irony?

Obliquely I recruited my boys, everywhere scouting and sifting.

Twice weekly I held workshops in my living room. The boys performed impromptu sketches and polished play scenes. I served small biscuitlike pizzas and cranberry punch, and after sessions we gossiped, or listened to stereo recordings of the Vienna Boys Choir. The true pulse of a campus can be felt in the prattle of these boys. They willingly confessed Krebler's caustic nickname (Mongoose); I extracted from them my own (Bison), and they disclosed that young Gwendolyn Dwyer "performed for the upperclassmen." I mentioned this last suggestive scrap of data to Ellie, but she failed to take it seriously. Had I followed *my* impulse and pursued the implications of "performed," I might well have prevented the mass humiliation of my own daughter.

But no, I was too engrossed in the cast selection for *Saint Joan.* I dispensed with the traditional method of selection, a schoolwide audition, and through my workshops painstakingly welded a viable troupe of gifted boys. A word of Michael Coldbrook, my Joan: what attracted me to the play was the wellspring of the heroine's power, her voices, and her enigmatic sexuality. Neither a virago, seductress, nor saint, my winning Jenny was the son of a widow who managed a potato farm in Aroostook, Maine. Savagely ragged by upperclassmen for his rich open-voweled accent, Michael retreated to the loneliness of the single room above my flat. His build was deceptive. He was slight but uncommonly vigorous. His skin had an agreeable windburned fervor. This, together with the chapped swell of his lips and his voice (which had yet to break) created an air of mildly abused wholesomeness. But what was most striking, I think, Michael was wall-eyed—simultaneously he seemed to watch you and elsewhere, to think worldly *and* unearthly thoughts. This was the ambivalent eye of one susceptible to visitations, of one who is a visualizer. When this young boy, dressed in the golden armor Ellie had fashioned, elevated his roving eye at rehearsals and said, "I dream of leading a charge, and of placing the big guns," one believed him.

9 *Dramatics, II.* I spent many cold evenings toward the end of March blocking scenes, scribbling notes on my clipboard. The production began to take shape, gained momentum through April when suddenly, the morale of the cast crumbled. Players mooned and skipped vital rehearsals. Michael dropped lines, became unruly, inattentive. Restlessness, impudence, a lovesick atmosphere was carried on the spring wind.

10 *Dramatics, III.* The last Sunday of April during a late rehearsal in Hamlin Gymnasium I picked my clipboard off a folding chair and read in gold-crayoned capitals:

BISON'S WIFE SCREWS MONGOOSE

For whatever reason I sat in the folding chair and feigned a calmness. For some minutes I considered the set. Downstage right Charles VII was propped on a lush canopied bed perusing *Boccaccio* and waiting for my cue to begin a run-through of the Epilogue. I ordered the entire cast to assemble on stage. After demanding the unknown author of the memo to remain, I canceled the rehearsal and dismissed the cast. Whooping and jostling, every boy left the gymnasium.

BISON'S WIFE SCREWS MONGOOSE—had the fingers of an Awful Hand printed "Mene, Mene, Tekel Upharsin" across my clipboard I should not have been more shaken. In each instance four terrible words presaged the division and fall of a kingdom and indicated its tyrant had been weighed in the balance and been found wanting. How is a man to respond to such knowledge? When suddenly the Master Puppeteer perceives subtle strings stitched into all his joints, what is he to do?

I stood reeling in the empty auditorium. Better, "Mongoose

Screws Bison's Wife," I thought while Dignity struggled with Rage and was thrashed soundly. To find them. To punish them. I recalled that the pool was used by faculty on Sunday afternoon. Lightheaded, my legs pumping with abnormal strength, I jogged up three flights of stairs to the spectator ramps. Below, Headmaster Dwyer, the lone occupant of the pool, floated on his back and sculled his white arms.

Outside the gymnasium it was already dusk. I drove to Hamlin Dormitory and stormed into my flat. The lovers were not there. Bayla was not there. Under the kitchen table was an empty cereal bowl. The film of milk inside it had not yet dried.

I climbed the stairs to Krebler's attic apartment. The door was unlocked. Like stalactites, dozens of abstract mobiles armed the ceiling. Its back ridged, Krebler's dog soundlessly hopped up and down sniffing my trouser legs. Otherwise the apartment was empty.

I turned on Krebler's desk lamp and inspected the contents of his desk. The bottom drawer was neatly compartmented: old issues of *Dog Parade Magazine* on the left, on the right various literary journals. Red-penciled themes were stacked in the top drawer. On the desk top was a small book in a glossy white dust jacket entitled *The Eye of the Vortex.*

I leafed through the book that was to change my life, and flipped it over to examine for the first time the face of the man who was to direct that change. Banok's temple rested on his bowed index finger, his contemplative eyes depressed. Under the photograph were the words "Author, Ponce Beach, Fla." I slipped the book into my sports coat, snapped off the light, and left the room.

11 *Dramatics, IV.* Seldom have I tried to reassemble the succeeding three hours and then, buffered by images, similes, and wild conceits. How else can the remainder of that frenzied evening be endured much less comprehended? And always the central image is water—the chemical turquoise water of the gymnasium pool where the lovers dallied and doubtless formulated their tricks; the brown water of melting snow streaming down the campus roadside gutters and filling every pothole; the saline water of my tears. It was as if I had spent my life constructing a great dike to dam all this flow when the keystone popped out, water sprouted, a fissure formed, torrents surged and I was washed away, waterlogged, sinking.

I have dreamed before of being suspended underwater in one of those hollow balls, a bathosphere; of suffocating, of being buried alive, of being born. I have read that the sea monster descried through the tinted porthole of my bathosphere, a serene long-necked monster resembling the prehistoric brontosaurus, could well be my own father's penis on it way to conceive me. Whatever, I do know I was reborn on that chaotic night.

I was spiraling, caught in an awesome funnel, a maelstrom— I drove my station wagon round and around the campus, past the classroom building, the church lit for Vespers, at first seeking Ellie and Krebler, then circling by momentum alone.

I was momentarily slowed while droves of boys, like bellicose nightwalkers, bacchantes, rioters, boiled out of the church portals into the spring night. I accelerated a half-turn around the campus and braked then swerved to dodge the phantom I assumed a cat. There followed a shriek, the sound skidding chalk makes on a blackboard. I jumped from my car and ran to the spot where Dash lay, legs still atwitch, head squashed on the asphalt. I was befuddled, stripped of the hunter's edge over the hunted. As if to accompany the temper of my thoughts a fierce Druidic chant reverberated through the warm air and though this chant seemed to originate across the campus, I distinctly remember supposing it an audial projection of my mental state. I carried the dead dog to the stone steps of the dormitory and plotted my next move.

Shortly, I was sitting, distraught, my head in my hands, staring at the dog's broken red snout, its little gravelly hide spread upon a newspaper on the kitchen table, when a fist offensively beat the door. "Pardon me," said the dapper mustached cleaver-headed man in the door chink, "but have you seen," and that instant, squinting peculiarly, his resemblance to the noxious Krebler ceased. Minutes before I should have throttled this man, such was my moral imperative. Now I meekly glanced down-ward as if I were reading that newspaper, such was the force of his. He folded his dog into a parcel of newsprint, sputtered, spat on my hairline, and the telephone rang.

A reprieve, I thought. But in fact, the ruffled blast of Head-master Dwyer's voice, nasilized by the receiver and so unlike his melodious fund-raising tones, cued the final vertiginous act of the evening. I informed Krebler the Headmaster had sum-moned me to his office. I apologized.

"This is far from over," he said bitterly. Bundle under his arm, he strode to the door and failed to close it. How right he was.

12 Untied.   The scene outside the Headmas-ter's door baffled me. To the left Michael Coldbrook along with some principles from *Saint Joan* bunched sulkily and silently. They did not greet me. The office door opened and there began a sorry procession led by two disheveled waifs caked with mud, the tops of their dresses torn, followed by a baleful Ellie and Headmaster Dwyer sporting our school's crested emerald blazer. Only then did I identify the ragamuffins as my daughter and the daughter of the Headmaster. Bayla had been weeping. My rush to her was blocked by the Headmaster's tense "Mr. Mabee," and I was ushered into his office. The inquiry of sorts was under way.

Inside, the Headmaster pinched his brow, exhaled deeply, and said, "I will be blunt. Did any of your seminars touch on the sub-ject of pagan ritual or sacrifice?" He coiled and uncoiled a pipe cleaner around his mahogany thumbnail. I assured him I had adequately explored these topics in connection with the theorized birth of tragedy. Succinctly I expounded on the ancient custom of killing a god in animal form, the ecstatic goat-song, the deep kinship of Dionysus with Pan and the Satyrs, the fire sacrifices of the Druids.

"Then you *did* teach them."

"I have certainly tried, sir."

"You *urged* them to perform these things," screeched the Headmaster, "Michael Coldbrook has confessed it." How different was this brutish inquisitor from that docile man floating on his back in the gymnasium swimming pool.

To this day I am dumbfounded. Urged them! But why? How could I be responsible? "Performed for the upperclassmen"— remembered, a gruesome phrase. Was I more guilty than the school chef who miscalculated the amount of saltpeter necessary to offset the spring thaw? Or the spring thaw itself? How could I have prevented my players from blindfolding giggling Gwendolyn and my daughter, from leading them behind the school building and under the oak tree? Could I have known Coldbrook would gather brushwood and start a bonfire in a sunken trashbarrel; call two tennis balls the testicles of Man, hurl them into the barrel mouth; that perhaps my own daughter and surely Gwendolyn were willing mock sacrifices, squealing each time a foreign palm packed their necks, chests, bellies, and slits with mud; that Headmaster Dwyer on leaving Vespers should hear their intoxicated moans, ambush the infidels under that oak tree, discover his frenzied half-clad daughter, capture them all, interrogate, and in the end, wanting for his daughter's promiscuity a scapegoat of stature—settle for Edgar Mabee?

All these questions became trivial once Ronald Krebler barged into the office, a tan shoebox held before him like an offering. His face was discolored as he placed the shoebox over the green blotter on the Headmaster's desk and lifted the lid. The grisly remains of Dash filled the cardboard coffin.

How could I counter Krebler's new wave of accusations? To the receptive Headmaster he maintained I had premeditated the murder of his Italian greyhound to avenge what I imagined his liasion with my wife. Furthermore, and most damaging, he insinuated my selection of Michael Coldbrook for the title role of *Saint Joan* was prompted by—he construed my feeling for Michael in a harsh and perverse light. By a freak of chance Krebler's concoctions were lent verisimilitude when he swooped at me and seized from the pocket of my sports coat *The Eye of the Vortex.* "To boot, he is a thief," the opportunist shrieked. I snatched back the book but already the Headmaster was swayed to Krebler's side.

Thus it was decided:

1 My biweekly seminars in theater were instrumental in provoking a primal scene, i.e., on my account Gwendolyn Dwyer was a thirteen-year-old tramp.

2 I vented groundless jealousy upon a dog.

3 I morally compromised a freshman boy.

4 I stole a book.

5 I was a self-seeking and incompetent director/teacher/proctor.

I was forced to tender my resignation. Michael was suspended pending psychiatric investigation.

And so, in all likelihood, my wife glutted Krebler's appetite. Coldbrook used my daughter.

My crime? Inadvertently I had crushed a miniature greyhound beneath a rear wheel of my station wagon.

Only now, half a year after my dismissal from St. Hubert's, can I say with candor that I forgive Michael and Krebler. Yes, I can forgive Krebler, but I curse forever his impoverished vision.

THE CUT WORM FORGIVES THE PLOW

Why? Though Krebler utilized my sense of humor, my love of game, I might almost add a certain innocence, to undermine my marriage; and though I have no doubt the tennis balls Michael shot into the fiery incinerator were surrogates for those folded in my own scrotum—still, they jointly christened the demolition of my loathsome former self.

I stated earlier I was reborn on that crazed night. With hindsight I see in Michael Coldbrook's pubescent ceremony my baptism by fire. But as the shiny new-skinned snake carries for a time the milky tissue of its molting skin, so I dragged to the Retreat a remnant of my old self.

Although my family had often summered at the Retreat in the past, we had never stayed during spring thaw. The ice had broken up in Rust Lake and rivers of melting snow preceded rivers of rain down the ridgeside. In the best of seasons Ellie had never been partial to the Retreat. She despised Julius, his love of hunting (it always amused her to contrast the quick haunches of a deer to Father's mammoth buttocks and chafing thighs), and his "man's man" lodge. The May afternoon Ellie slushed through the half-mile mud road to the Retreat, it was impossible to tell which was more darkly mired, the station wagon or my family.

13 *The Eye of the Vortex.* I decided to let sleeping dogs lie, and so mentioned neither Krebler nor Michael Coldbrook. But beware of sleeping dogs! Wife and daughter conspired to create a defensive arrogance, an arrogance founded on guilt and shame. Bayla became a specter of Ellie, charading her hostility, haughtiness, and sometimes, indifference. When I suggested that Bayla attend the final month of school in the village, she screamed, wept, and pouted. By treating Bayla as a companion, a confidante rather than a daughter, Ellie won her over, warped her, and set her on me. Not even for Bayla's sake would Ellie consent to share my bedroom. And I demanded so little from her. Normally, my modest flame was pinched out by the dual supposition I *could* have her, and no one else *was* having her. Normally, sleeping back to back sufficed me. But true to the mechanics of my decaying self, the probability of her numerous couplings with Krebler and her humiliating contractions at my approach sparked a hotter, higher flame.

So I kept to myself. Long walks on the lakeshore paths, canoe trips, swimming, and arduous study helped dull my anxiety.

June, July, to the day we left for Florida in August (the day following my first waking vision), there are few corporeal incidents to relate. The tumultuous happenings of this interim occurred inside me. The gradual emergence of my new self brought pain and longing I can scarcely describe. Who hears the shrill ululations of the husk, bursting from the pressure of a ripening ear of corn?

It is not unlike the throes of labor.

The Eye of the Vortex provided me a manual for a natural childbirth. The first half of this cryptic work completed the mosaic I had begun in my thesis, *The Prophetic Writer in English/American Literature.* And so very much more. For Banok supplied the enigmatic missing link of my thesis (the vortex), and dazzlingly compiled every eddy, whirlpool, whirlwind, gyre, cyclone, funnel, maelstrom, and vortex to be found in all of literature from Homer's Charybdis to the recondite diagrams of W. B. Yeats.

Some thousand vortex references—pearls strung on the gossamer of his commentary—led the reader to the boldly practical conclusions of the second half of *The Eye,* "The Three Steps." Here my former self was delineated and named (the *Shroud,* i.e., the illusory but dizzying descent into the funnel); at the funnel's still nadir my hitherto dormant being was restored in the form of the *Homunculus Divine,* the second of the three steps.

Where the *Shroud* coveted, the *Homunculus Divine* shared and forgave. While the *Shroud* wandered, incarcerated in a world of finite objects, the *Homunculus Divine* envisioned an infinity beyond the symbols and signs of the insubstantial material dungeon.

Beyond this second stage, however, I floundered until Florida. And I cannot yet say I firmly grasp how, once grown to maturity, the *Homunculus Divine*, this little man in the hollow of the vortex, can extricate himself totally from the whirling coils of the *Shroud*, leap upward, and become the third and ultimate step, the *Holy Androgyne*.

The tension between my new enthusiasm and my old domestic despair (between the *Shroud's* noose and the amnesty of the *Homunculus Divine*) became so lacerating by July's end that a single, exasperating yet symbolic incident made it imperative that I see Banok in the flesh: there was a cat, a tortoise-shell cat, owned, I assume, by summer people. For many consecutive evenings this green-eyed cat clung to our screen door and shrieked until Bayla served milk and table scraps. One dusk as I was musing beneath the maple tree this cat rounded the Retreat, a bluebird clamped alive in its paws. To rescue the bluebird and deprive the cat, or watch the bird be eaten? Close-by the cat crouched, apparently stalling to savor the kill, as cats do, or in need of some congratulatory gesture from me. The bluebird, his orange breast heaving, managed to free and desperately flutter one wing outside the cat's sharp mouth. Bayla came outdoors shortly with a shallow dish of milk. Perceiving the bluebird's situation, perceiving me observing this situation, Bayla threw down the dish and raged. I stamped threateningly and the tortoise-shell immediately spat out the bluebird and skittered into the birch grove. Bayla knelt by the bluebird who nested sluggishly on the lawn, his eyebeads inexplicable. Bayla picked him up carefully, but the damage had been done. Tiny sacks of organs protruded through his rusty belly. When Bayla discovered this, she began to abuse me. Bewildered, I took a rock and pressed the misery out of the little blue head. At this, Bayla struck me, fled indoors, and told Ellie I was stoning a bluebird to death. The instigating tortoise-shell, of course, never returned.

I had ceased to believe in my ability to effectively act. I seemed to clutch one horn of a dilemma, stretch myself to clutch the other horn, and be rammed senseless. This and more I described in the letter I posted air mail to Ponce Beach on the curled tip of Florida where, even then, my midwife was preparing his three-week seminar.

14 *Hambly.* I awoke to a raking on the door, the grating sound of a match on flint. I threw off the down quilt and looked out the frost-bordered window. Against the plastic pressed the large black nose, icy whiskers, and steaming muzzle of Hambly's long-snouted coonhound. From the corner of the orchard I spotted Hambly making his way toward me through the stiffened white field. He carried a shotgun and when he was closer I saw a limber rabbit, ears downward, dangle with the thrust of his thigh. I walked onto the porch. Hambly slipped the hind legs of the rabbit from his belt and held it up to greet me. "Early winter, Edgar. Rabbit's near to turned white already and the hornets' nests are high. An early one and a bad one."

Even if old Hambly is so rooted to the ground he's skeptical of clouds he can't see, I'm fond of him. First he slyly inquired if I had seen deer in the orchard; next he reminded me he had hunted the orchard and the woods around it for thirty years and only then, with a wink, did he ease into, "Mind if I scout around outside?" Such homely harmless wiles.

How could I have refused him? I can recall hiding under spruces with him years ago while my father waited like a stone idol. We would drink brandy-spiked coffee from the red plastic cap of his Thermos. How could I say no? Anyway I consented.

Before Hambly left, he bunched his gray whiskers in his fist and asked, "Ain't you goin' crazy up here?"

"The first few days," I confessed.

"Well, it's none of my business, Edgar, but I'd sure love to know what in Christ's name is goin' on."

"Simply," I explained, "Trying to reconstruct myself."

"Down below, I mean, at Retreat," said Hambly with a strange animosity. "What's with him, he ambidextrous or somethin'? Makes a man wonder who own this land, him or you?"

"Banok?"

"That hairy little fellow."

Annoyed, I said it made no difference.

"Sure as hell will to the selectmen at tax time."

What can one say to such stubborn literalness? My first visitor in over a week brings complications. Why this indignant attitude toward Banok?

It is incomprehensible Hambly should perceive merely a "hairy little fellow" ("ambidextrous" at that, whatever such an obscurely regional, albeit colorful adjective may mean to him.) I think poor Hambly suspects that Banok is after my lake property. Hambly and his landlocked senses.

DOES NOT THE EAGLE SCORN THE EARTH
AND DESPISE THE TREASURES BENEATH?

The eagle stares down the sun. The eyeless mole squeals from the weakest ray of light. By the nature of things, the mole in the pit shall resent the bold-soaring eagle.

How completely this notebook has tranquilized me. I look down on the Retreat and am startled by the changed landscape, sober and bare under a lesser sun. Perhaps the first snow isn't far off. In a funny way I feel embarrassed: I have been so absorbed, ruminating on the disintegration of my marriage, thinking of Ellie and Bayla and the rest, that I had forgotten all about them; or at least, my proximity to them.

15 Waking Vision.

> COME
>
> BANOK
>
> TARBELL RANCH, PONCE BEACH, FLA.

Such a long time my family had been adrift without a star or
distant horizon to give us bearing that the arrival of this concise
telegram, like an olive sprig in a pigeon's beak, set off quiet but
unanimous celebration. Ellie was bored, restive, wanted change.
Her desires, though neither so fierce nor directed as my battle
to dissociate my *Homunculus Divine* from the retarding lusts of
the *Shroud*, were negatively evinced in her glazed despondent
countenance. For in addition to our hapless marriage, her antipathy to the Retreat, her covert antipathy to Bayla, Ellie hated
the lake, alive now with the raucous speedboats of the
summer population. My presence continued to make her re-
coil—as before I was forbidden to touch her—but her indo-
lence miraculously lifted with the telegram's arrival. And simultaneously her Mimic stopped grumbling about nothing to do,
no decent playmates, not even a sailboat. So with an energy
akin to hysteria, a tenuously united family pitched in and prepared to travel south.

This functional harmony was, unsurprisingly, short-lived. Ellie
and Bayla retired early on the eve of the day on which our
journey was to commence, and left me to the humid night.
The lodge was stuffy. I stripped to my boxer shorts
and sat outside on the shore of the lake, peering into the milky
dark air. Heat lightning whitened patches of the sky. From the
cabins over the water murmurs carried, the vain tinkle of

glasses, a soft and voluptuous laugh. The hot air flashed and rumbled.

The withered *Shroud* is re-energized and thrives in such an atmosphere. It inflames the mind with longing and shoots illusory but potent shafts of heat down the spine to curl around the coccyx and settle in the loins. To combat the *Shroud* I employed exercises recommended in "The Three Steps": I plugged my left nostril and visualized the ejection of a scarlet stream of desire and disease from my right nostril. Out my left nostril I snorted a cobalt-blue stream of fear and anger. Three times out my rounded mouth I blasted purple lethargy, the inertia which had allowed the *Shroud* to gain its stranglehold.

The results of these exercises proved unsatisfactory. I slipped off my boxer shorts, plunged into the cool lake and zealously paddled about.

I am unsure of what transpired next.

There is a lapse, after which, undried, I found myself beside Ellie's bed. I had not willfully trespassed. That I swear. I had been driven to her room in a strangely automatic fashion. In a sense I had ceased to be Edgar Mabee; I had become the battlefield on which the *Homunculus Divine* clashed with the *Shroud* as ancient ice with fire.

Illuminated by that heat lightning, Ellie was never lovelier than outstretched there on her back. The bedsheet cast off in the heat split her in two. Her lax arm extended to the mattress edge where her wrist bent, fingers splayed slightly, wedding band tilted, cuticles ragged. The silvery floss of her visible labium stood on end as if electrified. One exposed breast melted into her lean ribcage. The attitude of her mouth I had never seen on her daytime face: she seemed on the verge of tasting an overheavy resinous fruit.

Suddenly, the lightning seemed actually to flicker through her bedside window, transforming the entire ceiling of the rough-beamed lodge into an iridescent placard engraved with the words:

BANOK ☀ ☀ ☀ OCULIST
DOCTOR OF THE INNER EYE

Where but an instant before Ellie had slept, Banok now sat grinding small lenses of glass. Glass dust glittered on the indigo woolen blanket like the Milky Way. On his flattened hand Banok held a prism up to my eyes. A rainbow appeared, one diaphanous base on his fingerpads, the other on the fleshy ridge of his palm. Banok's deep-contoured brow rested on his index finger, much in the manner of the photograph on the back cover of *The Eye of the Vortex;* but rather than the drab black-and-cardboard colors of the photograph, his strong face shone with golden health. From a small box Banok selected two glass needles and directed their points toward my eyes. His rumbling voice said, "This shall hurt but a moment in time. A moment of pain enables you to see all . . . ," but as the needlepoints were about to pierce my pupils (one flex of Banok's wrists, one short thrust would have climaxed my vision), Banok's luminous visage was suddenly deformed to the protuberant neck cords and eyes, the warped lips of Ellie's raving face. Her savage yell, "You sick bastard, you fucking pervert," blasted the sultry master bedroom with horror.

In this predicament, how could I have convinced Ellie she was only *half* right?

She had roused to a warm weak succession of salty splats on her cheek and eyelid, and that was enough for her. At once she spotted my organ receding into its wrapping of my fisted fingers. She saw my wet body loom exhausted above her.

No, my partial agreement with her vulgar invective could never have salvaged the situation. To Ellie, only the mean work-ings of the *Shroud* were apparent. And certainly the *Shroud is* sick, perverse, and degenerate. What more clear-cut proof of the *Shroud's* depravity can be had than the fact that at the very instant the *Homunculus Divine* led me into realms of vision, the *Shroud* coaxed my body into a mechanical self-abuse?

I retreated from Ellie's bedroom, bathed in the lake, and dressed. The remainder of that late summer's night I spent out-side, wandering in the birch stand behind the Retreat amidst a swarm of mosquitoes and questions. Was I culpable for the *Shroud*'s nastiness? Ought I nonetheless to capitulate? Would Ellie and Bayla still accompany me south? What did my vision signify? A confirmation of what? Was the tranquil lens-grinding figure of Banok an intimation of the *Holy Androgyne*? Had Banok already attained the third of the three steps? Would he like me? How could I set right Ellie's misconceptions?

Of two things I was sure:

1 Pain came not from a situation but from how one perceived the situation.

2 There could be no turning back. Alone if need be I would travel to Florida.

The night had taken its toll. The interrupted vision, the *Shroud*'s prank, the ugly aftermath, the buzzing rounds of questions: I was not really discouraged, but reduced, sapped of vital stamina.

When Ellie bounced out the door at sunrise, a pistachio-colored scarf around her throat and a merry smile on her face, I was aghast. "Awfully eager to leave, aren't you?" she said playfully. "Why don't you eat some breakfast first?" These pleasantries burned my ears with a venom more caustic than her malevolent epithets of the previous night. To pretend the paradoxical night had never been—this was treacherous derision. Yet the events I have just related actually did occur. Of this I am every bit as certain as that I once married Ellie.

16 *Banok, School, Fresh Fruit.* As much as I was gratified by Banok's visit, I am left in a quandary. Visits in general begin to pose a problem to my work, a stylistic problem, i.e., yesterday I was in bed, half-asleep, composing my first waking vision when Hambly's gun dog heralded Hambly; today my retrospective faculties were fixed on the journey down the Atlantic Coast and Banok's spry step hit the porch. Perhaps I should relegate all digressions to a rear appendix so the fluidity and power of my narrative will not be interrupted.

That I have written the above has suddenly filled me with self-disgust. Matters of style and the serious matter of reconstructing one's self make grotesque bedfellows. Whether I use my fingers, pliers, tweezers, whether I am anesthetized or alert, the point is to remove the deep-lodged quills of Memory.

Uncanny as it sounds, my perception of Banok remains substantially unchanged since the serene and feverish night of my waking vision, a night before I had yet to know him physically! Then, as now, he is elixir. When he is near, my muscular strength increases, my confidence, lucidity, and power all intensify threefold. What more can I say? He is a paragon of fused contraries, one of the nimble few who can climb the incorporeal ladder or descend the carnal ladder and happily arrive at the very same paradise of vision. How invigorating his visit was. And how good to see Bayla.

He came with gifts: a laundry sack of separately wrapped grapefruits and oranges, a necklace of figs, and the primary treat, a half-dozen fresh peaches. Vincent Tarbell Jr., his former student, sent them from Florida, and such is Banok's generosity, straightaway he brought a selection to High House.

"You are much leaner, harder," was his multileveled greeting as he clasped me to his chest in the doorway. Bayla was reticent, I might say timid, in her approach to me. She pressed my bearded lip lightly with her chapped wax-coated mouth and this very moment as I lift my lip to my nostrils I smell the faint perfume of her Chap-Stick. She sat on the floor by the woodstove and stared between Banok (sitting on the edge of my bed) and me (on the stool by the desk).

Bayla has a charming face when she broods. The stiff black tip of her braid, fanned by a red rubber band, looks like a large and expensive sable brush, undipped as yet in any paint tray. She remained silent until Banok tossed her the emptied laundry sack and asked her to fill it with apples in the orchard. She glared at Banok, the bag draped over her knees, and blushing said, "You do it."

How like her mother. Although I have softened Ellie's jagged features in Bayla's face and bestowed a robust sturdiness, I am afraid she has inherited her mother's mild nervous debility, a rash-prone too-expressive coloration. Banok skipped across the room, squatted, touched her hands, whispered, and lo, a transformed girl rose to gather apples.

How does he do it? A few soothing words, slow dynamic gestures, an uncluttered eye—really, I don't know. The change to colder weather had given her a head cold, Banok said, she was out of sorts. Banok himself looked a bit peaked. His tan has faded but he was absolutely rippling with projects and ideas.

It is difficult to imagine that by next summer High House will be a school with naked children romping, scrambling out of doors to plunder the orchard or to weed a large organic garden. A genuine school, Banok said, where children and children, parents and parents, children and parents, parents and children, where, in a word, *Relationships* are the sole splendid pieces of educational equipment. He envisions the day when Doctors of Chemistry will quit their tenured positions to push wheelbarrows and, together with Doctors of Literature, create measured compost heaps for gardens of health. Children will be our instructors. Mature women will tie up their long hair with rawhide, eschew deodorants, and as men do, let their body hair express itself. Then unafraid, naked children *of all ages* will confront themselves and one another in a living experiment: natural childbirth, breast feeding, organic gardening, honesty—a sane unpoisoned era of one free collective soulbodymind is dawning, and if properly manured, will grow to a proud fruition on the very spot where I write these words!!

Banok is not dreaming. If I know him, he will stop at nothing and it will come to pass. He thinks his objectives are shared by others who have fled the city: artists, musicians, poets, writers, scientists, educators: men, women, and children of quality—the hills surrounding the lakes are packed with them, and Banok is one to harness such power.

Unbearable compassion drives him to these plans. He recounted to me a story he had overhead in the village of a thirteen-year-old boy waiting for the school bus on a country road not far from Rust Lake. A doe had crossed the road one hundred yards away and become snared in barbed wire loosely strung between cedar posts. This boy ran up to the deer, noosed now in the barbed wire (a boy one year Bayla's senior), took out his pocketknife, and slit the doe's throat. He ran back to his farm to notify his mother of his luck, and while the deer's heart pumped the last of its blood from the throat hole, the youth boarded the school bus, books in his armpit.

"Is the sort of school that nurtures this cast of mind tolerable?" Banok lowered his head, screwed up his lips, shook his head, and sharply snapping his fingers with the remembrance, added, "Hambly stopped by last week. He wanted permission to kill animals on the property. Rather than send him to you, I sent him packing. I know you would have done the same."

Bayla was dawdling under an apple tree. She waved. "Enjoy the fruit," Banok shouted, halfway across the orchard. He met Bayla, heaved her partially filled sack over his shoulder, and reconciled, they started hand in hand down the slope.

"I know you would have done the same." Why didn't Hambly plainly say that Banok had denied him hunting privileges? I will rescind the permission I gave Hambly. I will explain to him that he can no longer trespass.

17 The Journey. I shall resume my story without contrivance, with integrity.

And so, we drove to Florida. Ellie insisted she drive the station wagon.

I have no need to conceal a transition. What is a transition but a joint, like the joint of Ellie's gaunt shoulder, her bare arm propped on the steering wheel. That whole trip south I dozed against the car window, now and again narrowly opening my lids to focus on the blue bristle of her armpit. She has not shaved to this day, I venture.

Thirty-two years old, and this was my first excursion outside the boundaries of New England. And now I was on my way to Florida to study under Banok. The dreams I dreamed on that ride. How hot the station wagon became. After the mid-point of the journey the heat actually made me nauseous. I begged Ellie to stop so an air-conditioner might be installed, but on and on she drove. She seemed to relish the humidity. Excessive heat has always bothered me, the ugly sensation of my shirt sticking to my spine. The sun was altogether different from the New England sun. And the light, like snow glare, in summer. I forced myself to eat at the highway restaurants: hearts of lettuce and cheese sandwiches.

Farther south the car became a swelter. Opening the window offered no relief. The air cauterized my nostrils. Cartoons of Southern Florida, the golden Keys, crowded my brain. Swollen porpoise lips. Lime-colored lizards with skins of crepe. Ruby pomegranate cells in a crimson parrot's beak. Bashful Gauguin youths with fragrant black hair, sunlight skins, sucking milk from the coconut. Ponce de León slicing an infinity of Carboniferous ferns with his feeble machete. And myself, Edgar Mabee, one of grim Hawthorne's New England flower bulbs, about to be transplanted to prolific Italianate soil. What opulent swollen specimens bloomed there under Hawthorne's black thumb . . . immodest fuschia and mauve orchids, gigantic, gorgeous, viscous . . . Southern Florida . . . so fertile . . . and Banok. A Celestial Hothouse.

Whenever Ellie pulled off onto the highway shoulder to unfold a road map or parked along the moat of one of those plastic castles where doubleted attendants serviced our car and waitresses wearing coned sorcerer's hats dispensed hamburgs within, the luscious images of my trance dispersed, snoring

Bayla slowly revived, and Ellie smiled at me as at another mother's infant. She has not directed a harsh word to me since the night before our departure. But there was no love in that smile.

Midnight, a day's drive from our destination, Ellie selected a motel with an adjoining diner. Against all logic the setting of the sun did not cool the air. The night was ruthless. The diner had closed minutes before. Ellie hammered on the curtained glass door and finally a long finger pinched back the curtain and a slim black man with a red clip-on tie looked into her face. He made no expression but let us in.

I sat on a stool before the aluminum counter and listened to my headache. A fan whooshed hot fried air into my face, turned away, and whooshed again. Bayla sat beside me and requested a dime to play music. I refused. Ellie settled next to Bayla. A mirror running the length of the wall behind the counter made it unnecessary to glance sideways at Ellie. To spite me, the black man took a coin from the register and slid it into the jukebox. What with the reheating grill and the music, the diner was hotter than outside.

"No rush to order, no hurry now," the black man said from Ellie's side of the counter. He snapped off his tie, opened his shirt and drummed long fingers on the orangeade cooler.

I saw in the mirror exactly how it happened: Ellie leaned forward on her elbows and inspected a menu. The top three buttons of her blouse had come undone, and even from my stool the seamed cups and delicately laced border of her bra were exposed to the mirror.

I nudged Bayla to get Ellie's attention. Ellie looked ahead to where my reflection pantomimed a buttoning procedure up my shirt.

None of this I am sure escaped the black man's expressionless (or if not expressionless, no expression I knew anything about) gaze. Ellie nodded to me and rounded her lips in peeved comprehension. Rapidly she unbuttoned the remainder of her blouse, freed the tails from the waist of her skirt, and I swear, like a woman opening shutters to the morning sun, flung open her blouse!

The black man continued drumming on the sweating orange cooler. Ellie's swaggering eyes met my eyes in the mirror. Her head turned directly toward him. Even Bayla grinned. Pungent and low his laughter broke and to the tempo of the hiccoughing laughter of Ellie's body, the black clapped his oversized hands.

I ate nothing in that diner, but I learned an enormous truth about Ellie to compensate, and namely: she embraced neither the dew of the earth nor the fat of heaven; she embraced only the reflection of her own individuality; her smile was a frozen smile of aggression, her lover the *Shroud* which immured her. Desperately she retained obsolete conceptions of me, for I was a changed man and my transformation had widowed her. And in the end I poignantly realized that unconsciously Ellie had journeyed south for salvation, that she too craved Banok's help.

18 *Confrontation.* No sooner were the last of my peaches consumed for dessert, the kettle filled in the shallow spring behind the house, the water at a boil, and camomile set to steep, than close-by I heard one rifle shot, and another. Hambly. I had no doubts. Still, a confrontation promised to be disagreeable. I hesitated.

It is odd how an uncontaminated eye can transmute an ordinary object, refuse even, to an inspirational emblem, but this was the case when I thought on the six peach stones on the corner of my desk—six tiny maroon brains huddled together to form one great communal brain. Perhaps it was sentimentality, but I saw myself, Banok, Ellie, Bayla, Lynn, and Dot represented in that assembly (had there been but one stone more for baby Robin, the symbol was perfect).

Emboldened, I rushed behind the house and loudly shouted Hambly's name. We practically collided. Puffing like some worn coursing hound, his blood roused, Hambly blurted, "Good-size buck—go two-twenty I bet—missed once then got'm in the ass—he went down—jumped up and took off."

Those six reddish peach-stones and Banok's phrase, "I know you would have done the same," fortified me. I told him to leave the property at once.

"I said I hit him in the ass, Edgar. He'll off an' die, you know as well as me he will."

I held firm. Hambly was an infamous liar. The stories he told me when I was a boy. I am certain he shot no buck. I would have no animal butchered on my land; I stressed this point.

"What in Christ's name's got into you, huh?" He said that over and again. I had no choice but to order him off the property. He stood there, incredulous, nodding back and forth. I pointed out he was now a trespasser.

"That's a ton a meat to rot somewhere," he said, unloading his rifle, "it makes me puke." As the moralist is wont to do he took a parting swipe—"You're the bootcher, Edgar, not me"—and he slouched off into the woods the way he had come.

I do not condemn Hambly. I dissociate his ignorant and brutish State from the Individual. Hambly is in the State of the Hunter. All the day he scours the hills or scans between trees in search of something to kill. And he is happy! If only he knew what delusion such happiness is. Hambly is crossing the ocean in a make-believe boat. Can't he see this is impossible?

I do not condescend to the *real* Hambly. That Hambly I love. It is the Hunter I abhor. And the world is full of Hunters, one of the many costumes of the protean *Shroud*.

I am reminded of the group of construction workers repairing a culvert at the entrance of the Ponce Beach Seaquarium. I had Ellie stop and I rolled down the window to ask them the location of either Banok's school or the Tarbell residence. One brawny-jawed Hunter with a pickaxe glanced at my New England license plate and said, "You travel this whole way to see the Swami?" His mates bent lewdly to glimpse Ellie, Bayla, or both.

The "Swami" or as Hambly said, the "ambidextrous fellow" —Florida or Maine—the State, the dearth of vision, is one and the same.

19 *Ponce Beach.* The start of the long summer's-end dusk, the spearlike shrub clusters that lined the circular drive to the Tarbell ranchhouse, the silver and green palm shadows on the baked roof tiles, the chameleon that rakishly wiggled up the stucco wall and behind an aluminum hurricane awning, the sun-red cove beyond, that momentous first sight of Banok—at long last my destination had been reached.

A muted welcome answered my knock and I opened the door. In the sunken kitchen to the left a shirtless young man with a blue terrycloth towel around his waist was cooking fish. A wan blond girl burped a newborn infant before the picture window looking out on the cove. An older chunky woman was asleep in a rope hammock over the brick patio on the right.

The young man flipped over the fish with a spatula and sheepishly, Vincent Tarbell Jr. introduced himself. His lean brown chest was bumpy with cartilage and his sun-streaked auburn hair, drawn into a ponytail, fell limp between his shoulders. A jade disc hung on a gold wire from his right earlobe. He offered us some red snapper. Ellie and Bayla were famished and accepted. I was too excited. The older woman lowered herself from the hammock and grumblingly retired further into the house. The blonde meekly said hello, that she was Lynn, her son Robin.

"Banok is swimming," Vincent said. Sliding glass doors opened to the patio and beach. I ran down a wooden ramp to a thatch-roofed beach hut without walls and scanned the scarlet horizon. I rushed to the edge of the shore.

A compact dark shape grew slowly out of the water. Dusky and regenerate, like some D. H. Lawrence god emerging from centuries of sleep in a Mexican sea, Banok swayed from side to side as he made his way to the beach. He ejected a forceful geyser from the tip of his snorkel, slid his black pinocchio mask onto his forehead and slapped toward me on massive black-webbed feet.

"Edgar," he said in such a way as made clear he knew far more than my name. He held out his hands, and when I thought the greeting over and loosened my grip, he grasped my hands more firmly and smiled. Waterdrops caught in his coily black chest hair glistened like rubies in that setting sun.

Then and there we knew we loved each other. I could tell by the spinal shiver his tightened grip produced, by a tender light of empathy in his deep-socketed dark eyes—we were blood brothers and would henceforth share everything, give up anything for the other.

20 *The First Day.* I woke late the next morning on the patio cot. The husky older woman was eating half a grapefruit at the top of the kitchen stairs and watching me. "Don't mind me. I double as maid and fool," she said. She also informed me that Ellie was on the beach with Bayla, Banok had driven to Miami to meet one Jesse Staple's flight, and that she was Dot, Banok's wife. This last astonished me. She was so willful, abrupt, vulgar. I had never imagined Banok married. Somehow he seemed a marriage all by himself.

I have never been able to understand Dot. Is she jealous of Banok, resentful? Scornful? Or has she a twisted sense of the comic (no one else laughs when she does. Hers is a bizarrely private humor—a continuous bad joke). She embarrasses me and I can't distinguish whether I am confounded by her or ashamed for her. Really, I don't see where she fits in. I asked her where I might change into my bathing suit.

"Right where you are," Dot said, squeezing the grapefruit over her serrated spoon and staring directly at me. So I did, and hastened outside to where Bayla was engaged in a horseshoe match with Vincent in the shade. Ellie lay on a beach towel nearer the water. There was a wind off the cove. The sand was hot on my feet and looked like ground bone. I walked up to her quickly. Her bra was unhitched and her gold panties were so low the cleavage of her buttocks extended beyond the tight elastic waistband. I said nothing. She mumbled for me to step aside, that I was blocking the sun, and for once, she turned the other cheek.

I tried to make the best of that first day. I took a brief swim, played a game of horseshoes with Vincent (he told me his father was THE Vincent Tarbell, fruit and cattle magnate), and visited Ponce Beach Seaquarium with Bayla. Rays and sharks, a fanged eel and a sea turtle spent their gloomy days in the tanks below the concrete amphitheater, but all their flapping and gliding failed to hold Bayla's attention. Above, however, the porpoise and seal extravaganza captivated her. A tanned white-haired lady in a sailor's cap and a navy-blue swimsuit hung over a high diving board and shook little fish. One and two porpoises flashed around the pool and synchronously leapt, hovered, and gently accepted the proffered fish.

Bayla marveled (how long since I had heard that silly happy laugh of hers?) at the obese seal that toddled up to the poolside, squeezed "My Country 'tis of Thee" on the varicolored bulbs of brass horns, and fiercely applauded itself and barked. Twice she watched the entire show. The concrete tiers cooled my back and baked my front. I realized I had not been alone with Bayla in years. I put my arm around her shoulder. "This is really fun," I said. Bayla looked at me in the oddest way, ducked under my affectionately extended arm, and falteringly expressed her desire to go swimming. Nothing rankles like a child's suspicion. She was ill-at-ease with her father and it hurt me deeply.

Her swimsuit was underneath her blouse and shorts and she

bolted toward the beach almost before I parked the car at the ranch. Slumped in an orange canvas deck chair under the thatch hut, Vincent played a recorder. I took off my short-sleeved shirt and shoes and kept watch of Bayla. She ran full speed into the lucent water, belly-flopped, and crept ashore to do it again.

A frail young woman in slacks opened the sliding glass doors and joined me. She began to talk the moment I noticed her—"Isn't it lovely here?"—as if to distract me from the dorsal fin that ridged her jersey and misshaped her shoulder. Her face was young independent of her body and I had no idea how old she was. Shrilly enthused, she launched a discussion of Banok's *Eye of the Vortex*. Evidently she and Banok had talked of it on the ride to Ponce Beach. It was not that the uncomprehending reviewers had discouraged him, that was not why he would never again write, she said: rather, he had become intrigued with film for metaphysical and medicinal reasons. He had demolished the frequent charge that his book was derivative by stating simply, "Genius is in the finding, not the object found."

Jesse Staple awaited the start of the seminar with a need equal to my own. When she sighted Banok, small in the distance, strolling around the edge of the cove with Ellie, her eyes became animated, her speech more rapid. "He is the most alive man I have ever seen," she said.

21 *Seminar Begins.* The sun had done its work on me. My skin became the terrible shade painters call "alizarin." As in those "Imagination" plates of Daumier, horned goblins and tailed demons had chafed rattailed files on my neck and shoulders, singed my eyelids, nostrils, and ears, hacked and sawed at my ankles: in short the sun had crippled me. Alternately I was afire and frozen. I could neither eat nor walk.

Dot scoffed and coated my burned parts with Vaseline. Lynn

drifted in and out sheerly clothed, a tumbler of iced tea with a lime wedge in one hand, screaming Robin in the other. Ellie was gone the majority of the day with Bayla. Banok too was gone, busy in the darkroom or off preparing the opening session of the seminar for later that evening.

Wild itchings seized me at nightfall. I wrapped a sheet around my body but it stuck to the Vaseline. Never had I so desired to peel off my skin, emerge from my body, and be free.

How I labored to concentrate on Banok's introduction. His seminar was to last three weeks: a Week of Dialogue, Week of Film, and Week of Organic Language. My greased eyelids hurt to keep open. Banok sat in a rattan chair before two stubby candles. Vincent sat crosslegged on a straw mat beside him; then Lynn and Jesse closed the circle. Dot nested in the hammock. Robin, Bayla, and Ellie were in other rooms, asleep, and I, facing Banok, strained to keep alert on my cot.

Banok talked of the *Shroud* and Language. He said we were degraded, confused, fawning, because we obeyed a divisive and devious master, Language. My itching made it impossible to follow all the subtle and speedy turns of his thought. Generally, though, he said, we cannot imagine, cannot think, cannot speak but we are confined within the pale of Words. Whenever we reach a dead-end, when we can see no further, there we discover a Word and the Word says, "I am the boundary of the World." For the next three weeks we would strive together to raze this boundary, to overthrow repressive Language and once again become proud, playful, and united.

Vincent said, "But I see . . ."

"Stop," said Banok calmly. "Here is the perfect illustration. This 'I' that 'sees,' Vincent, where is it located? In your ears? (Banok touched Vincent's ear.) Chest? Does it reside in your eyes?"

"Well, in a mirror I . . ."

"Stop. Reflected eyes see no more than the nose in the same mirror. And where does Vincent's 'I' lead us? Follow this chain of death: 'I' denotes a discrete subject. Implicit is the existence of an object. 'I's do things, are doers. They are distinct from the deed done. Already this 'I' is isolated from the world, from other 'I's. 'I' is inside Pandora's Box. In truth, Vincent sees 'dash', Vincent has the thought 'dash', Vincent believes 'dash', Vincent says 'dash', are all precisely the same as 'dash' sees 'dash'. What Vincent sees is Vincent. Vincent sees and therefore *is* Jesse and Edgar and Lynn and Dot (like a spider up in her webbed hammock, Dot at this point said, "No, thank you") and me and these candles and the hammock and the ceiling, the ocean, the sky . . . Our revolution will be built on the death of Language. But how can we employ Language to destroy Language? By turning it on itself, and as the Serpent circles to devour its tail, middle, and head, Language will be no more."

I passed the next days indoors. My skin blistered and there was no comfort. Through the sliding glass doors I scored horse-shoe games or lazily followed beach play. Lynn accompanied me inside and attended Robin, leafed through yarn samples and pattern catalogues, and worked her small loom.

The linguicide Banok plotted commenced as one by one we told our story. For the next four days we unburdened ourselves and, gradually, we grew intoxicated on the candor of our confessions, and instead of shame there was a burgeoning rapture.

22 Vincent Tarbell Jr. I was mystified by one of Banok's techniques. He distributed red crayons and rolls of paper and instructed us to scribble on the paper whenever we spoke. Mornings, he would privately interpret the markings: "Markings, if read correctly, are more revealing than the spike-waves of encephalography." Banok drew the words from us. Sympathetically, he primed us and silently absorbed our exposures.

Prior to our arrival Banok had begun curative measures with Vincent (a filmed fantasy to be shown during the Week of

Film). Consequently, Banok asked Vincent to begin, to share the traumatic significance of the *Life-size Human Head*. At first I thought Vincent was going to come apart. He grew flustered, lit a cigarette, and toyed with his jade earring. After a long pause he picked up a red crayon, pressed out his cigarette, and with diffident softness, said, "It all started because I wanted to be a doctor. I was eleven. Lydia, my mother, bought me a microscope and boxes and boxes of stained protozoa slides. She bought a stethoscope too, a bag of instruments, and a real sphygmomanometer. Sometimes in the evenings I would wind its heavy rubber around my proud Dad's arm and take his blood pressure. But what infatuated me the most was the *Life-size Human Head*, this plastic model I loved to assemble and take apart. There was a transparent skin case, detailed decals for retinas, a green pituitary bulb, separate teeth, optic nerve tubing, and a pink brain. The cerebellum was one solid piece; the lobes of the cerebrum were composed of four pieces—two bulging convoluted outsides and two flat striated insides where the right and left lobes were to be fitted together. I never did glue the lobes together though, for inside each lobe was a cavity, and there I hid my most secret things.

"You see, I lied to my mother when I told her my new ten-speed bicycle had been stolen. Actually, I swapped it with this kid at school for a snapshot, a three-by-five-inch color snapshot of his aunt taken in the Everglades by his uncle, an amateur photographer. She was naked on a mossy cypress stump and bent over backward so I couldn't see any face. The camera had been clicked so close to her vagina that it looked like one big red scalp wound inside of another. I stored the snapshot inside the right cerebrum of my *Life-size Human Head*. I lived petrified it might be discovered, but my fear was overcome by the happiness I felt whenever I perused the picture, a strange feeling worth a thousand ten-speed bicycles.

"The contents of the left cerebrum's cavity gave me even greater dread and a more delirious joy. My addiction began one day when I was carrying a bag of trash to the garage. I noticed this cylinder of aluminum foil. Inside I found two dead-black cottony sticks with fuses, likes dynamite.

"I smelled them. The odor was piercing and unforgettable.

"I smelled them again and again.

"I coveted these enigmatic sticks, often rummaged the garbage, and in a few months had collected a dozen or more. Soon the left cerebrum couldn't hold another. I would lock my bedroom door, prop the snapshot on the base of the *Life-size Human Head* and sniff the mystical sticks or lightly touch one with the flexed tip of my tongue. If one particular stick lost its incense, and they all did in time, I disposed of it and substituted a fresh one in the tight-packed left lobe.

"Through ratiocination I suppose, at fourteen, I came to the shriveling conclusion that these sticks I so frequently inhaled and fondled were my mother's discarded *tampons*.

"I felt doomed. I threw away every one. But before a month passed by, like a destiny, the left lobe was filled to capacity. My indulgence has stalked me through the years. Relationships with women, of course, have proven futile. How could I hope to achieve transports comparable to my bliss behind locked doors? Always the possibility my fetish might be discovered has added that extra fuel.

"The whole situation worsened about a year ago. I was sleeping in the sun, on the beach, when involuntarily I sat erect. Ten yards away a woman in her late thirties was trotting along the shore. My fetish had sharpened into a sixth sense—the gifted nose of the canine to pick up the scent of a bitch in heat. As surely as any mongrel dog knows, I knew from the spoor of that lady in the skirted bathing suit. Unable to quit her trail or accost her, I followed three or four miles along the ocean. She became aware of me, stopped and turned to ask what I wanted. How could I explain? What words could I use? Has any man the courage to beg a woman to lay down in a palm grove so he might smell her thoroughly? I fell to my knees like a victim of common sunstroke, and before she fled, afraid of what would be taken from her, I had already managed to take the fill of my lungs. If she had known the desires I harbor, if the man on the street knew of the fantasies . . ." and here Vincent broke off, sweating.

His crayon half what it was when he began his confession (I saw the acute peaks and dips on his roll of paper), Vincent's eyes turned inward and his shoulders bounced convulsively.

Banok cradled his head and rocked from knee to knee. He brushed Vincent's auburn hair from his face and said, "People will see. They will see that your dream is but a metaphor of their own dreams. That I promise you. Only be patient. Wait until your film."

23 *Jesse Staple.* Banok was not always this tender. I was repulsed by his swift and violent response to the harrowing story Jesse Staple related. Only afterward, when I had grasped his distinction between *salubrious*, or *creative* aggression and the Hunter's aggression, did I fathom the wisdom of his shock compassion. With admirable concision Banok had said, "Passive Pity wrings fingers and toes. Compassion swoops."

Jesse spoke with celerity, as if she were allotted only so much time and wanted to include everything. Several times she watched her thin hands and Banok had to remind her to utilize her crayon/paper device. Whereas Vincent's story, like a story told often before, was nicely paced and roundly constructed, Jesse's began, strayed, panicked, continued, accelerated, and digressed.

I simply lack the skill to render her asymmetrical tale—its sadly acerbic tone and frantic episodic quality which but shadowed her crooked spine. Nonetheless, I have decided to employ a largely third-person narration to intimate something of her technique and the scene's eerie quality: And when she finally was invited to dinner by an intern she met in a hospital cafeteria; accepted; dined—he slid his hand under her light back brace, said he had enjoyed her company, and went right for it. They all did, she said, all went right for it. The artist who wanted to catch the "flippancy in her eyes" begged her to first strip to the waist. The biology instructor probed as they waltzed in his two-room apartment. It became impossible to stop them. And why should she? And how? With a slap, with wit, with sorrow? She let them have their way They introduced her to so many others. A metaphysician in graduate school with one pragmatic eye proposed some sort of "financial arrangement" to be kept discreetly within his philosophic coterie. No one talked directly of her deformity and no one handled it with affection.

She had spent the past year in Mexico trying to teach in a strange land, to be with children. Whenever she walked through the slums of Cruillas, bands of swarthy urchins straggled behind her, imitated her irregular gait, and squawked, "Camel, camel."

"These were not children," Banok said.

"All were under ten."

"Indoctrination," smiled Banok heavily. "These were not children but old dying men and women. Childhood, remember, is a manner of seeing, non-verbal and non-causal."

Old or young, they congregated at dusk beneath the balcony of her flat and caroled, "Camel, camel, camel, camel." Jesse chanted herself into a fit of laughter. In a flash, Banok "swooped" behind her. He ripped up the back of her blouse, unhooked her therapeutic halter and lavished fierce kisses on the ridge of her dorsal fin. Jesse screamed under the first touch of his lips as under a scalpel. Banok signaled to us (Jesse could not have seen this), and one at a time we kissed her hard cartilaginous ridge. Jesse covered her face and shivered. Her laughter ceased. Her small breastless nipples stuck out like the rubber teats of a baby's bottle. From that instant her nervous loquacity vanished. Banok had chosen the precise moment and as a result, in one terrific paroxysm, Jesse achieved the serenity that had for a lifetime eluded her.

24 *The Man Who Was Rid of the Shroud.*
Unfortunately, I offered nothing so localized and tangible as
Vincent's morbidly keen olfactory sensibility or Jesse's disfigured
spine. Mine was a disease of perception, and to effect a cure,
Banok employed all the skill of the anti-linguist, the poet-
philosopher, the therapist, the midwife, the oculist—and when all
fell short, he gave himself, consummately.

Though not so sumptuously documented as my present remi-
niscence and not nearly equal in human interest to the sensa-
tional happenings disclosed by my seminar fellows, my story at
the least provided Banok with tools for an exploratory. He took
special interest in me and often we took long morning walks together.

The sixth day of the Week of Dialogue, Dot took Bayla to
explore a nearby Spanish fortress and Ellie joined us by the
thatch hut, her skin soft and brown as leather well saddle-soaped.
We all walked the beach (my skin had peeled and as a precau-
tion I carried a parasol) to the lighthouse on the point, a distance of two miles.

"All the symptoms of the *Shroud* are present," Banok told me
that morning. "Jealousy, intolerance, inhospitality, a vengeful
and judgmental nature."

"I've known that for years," said Ellie as she kicked foam
from the edge of the water.

"Your sole occupation should be the consideration of these
symptoms. And alone. You must start at once or else the
Homunculus Divine will have no room to grow."

"Judge? But whom do I judge?" I asked Banok.

"Me," interrupted Ellie.

"Only children and dogs judge in Utopia, for they alone do not
err," said Banok. "I once knew a man, a teacher, totally rid of
the *Shroud*. He returned home one chilly night and discovered

his wife with her lover, asleep in the bedroom. A light was on and nothing covered their nakedness. So banal, this situation is nonetheless archetypal, the touchstone of countless philosophies, murders, jests, and novels. But the man I knew spread a sheet and blanket over the exhausted lovers' bodies so they would not be cold. He turned off the light so they should sleep well. That evening he prepared refreshments for them. This was not weakness but Vision. Measure yourself, Edgar. Could you do the same?"

From the lighthouse on the point we could see the new nine-story Ponce de León Condominium rising, it seemed, from a foundation of turquoise water. Banok pointed over the water toward this imposing structure and said, "Wealthy people live in that condominium. They live in separate suites. An elevator brings them up and takes them down. They swim in heated pools instead of in the ocean. Couples live separately and bicker about health and adultery and they golf and play bridge. Imagine instead, Edgar, that across the water is one giant Human Body. The elevator is its digestive system. The electrical system is a net of nerve fibers. The quarrelsome people are actually corpuscles streaming here and there through the body. Their glamorous suites are the various organs. I tell you Edgar, if you are able to see one giant Human Body over the water, you have imagined a microcosm of the world. For the entire world, animate and inanimate, *is* one giant Human Body. The tragedy is that this giant chooses to see itself as a vast apartment building composed of a myriad separate fragments. You and Ellie and I are but fats, nerves, and proteins, infinitesimal components of the selfsame body. That, Edgar, is Vision. That giant is the *Holy Androgyne.* How can one be jealous, possessive, and judgmental? Does the thumb possess the forefinger? If I touch your wife and something in you balks, something is jealous, be sure the *Shroud* is alive within you. For is the capillary jealous of the artery? I think you understand the absurdity of such a question."

25 *The Blueprint.* The final night of the Week of Dialogue, Vincent was spiteful and garrulous. The Week of Film was to open the next night with the premiere of Vincent's major recurrent dream sequence. Jesse sat without agitation, ever listening, seldom speaking. Her turbulent quest was over. Repeatedly Vincent badgered Banok as to how he would implement his ideas in society at large. Banok explained that when the stuff of individual life is peaceful and sensuous and playful, so too will be the stuff of society. "If you see aright," he said, "the individual eye *is* the eye of all the world."

But Vincent could not be pacified. He grew wary, constipated, scratched the backs of his hands. He demanded greater proof.

Before we went to bed, Banok told us a story of how one revolution *had* come about. His story (at once a fairytale and a blueprint for action) was so lovely, simple, and significant and Banok spoke it with such stately ease that each word impressed itself on my brain like a signet in warm wax.

"One evening in the middle of the sixteenth century a stranger, wearied by his long northern journey over the mountains from Italy, rested his mule by the ruin of a monastery and gazed down on the circular wall of a small village. Rising high over the village in the center of the stone circle were the turrets of a great castle. The stone front of the castle glowed orange and yellow from three enormous bonfires. Until he rode down the slope to the village wall the stranger could not smell the stink of burned human flesh and hair nor hear the lamentations.

"An armed sentinel above the gate refused him entrance. 'My orders are that no one shall enter this day.' Something in the bearing of the stranger unsettled him and he asked the stranger to wait and ran along the walltop and down the massive steps to fetch the castellan.

"The black-bearded castellan was a gruff and callous man. 'What is your business here?' he shouted.

" 'I have no business,' the stranger said. 'I am Schamir the Physician and I am tired.'

"At this the castellan started, for he was an ambitious man. He clattered along the walltop and down toward the castle. After some minutes he returned to the battlement above the gate and said, 'Fürst von Kisslegg, lord of this village, welcomes you to rest the night in his castle.' Schamir bowed his head and the heavy wood and metal door was slowly pushed open. A young groom led Schamir's mule through the hot smoke-filled courtyard. Three black and smoldering piles were each watched by five or six people wrapped in black cloth. They wept and moaned, huddled to give one another comfort. In the rubble Schamir noticed the charred and shriveled form of a child.

" 'But what could they have done?' asked Schamir with sadness.

" 'The falling sickness,' whispered the groom timorously and said no more. He led Schamir's mule to the stable beside the castle. A small quick-eyed man, a black hood on his head and a long black cloak over his shoulders was waiting there.

" 'I am Hornberg, Finder for the Fürst von Kisslegg,' the small man said, examining Schamir as one might an egg for a crack. Satisfied, Hornberg said, 'Follow,' and wheeled about with a twirl of his cloak.

"Guards averted their eyes when Hornberg passed. Servants scurried into the darkness between torches. 'The people are frightened,' Hornberg explained, 'because some in the village have been seized by the falling sickness. Yesterday a nine-year-old boy fell spitting in the market place. Two of his playmates had been infected. Fourteen thus far have been burned and I fear the village has not yet been delivered of the demons.'

"Through the damp narrow corridors Schamir followed. At last they arrived at a room high in the castle where a man with dark-circled eyes stared abstractly through a lancet into the smoldering courtyard below. A white-haired girl knelt beside him, her face buried in his lap. Hornberg entered without announcement. The weary-eyed man shielded the girl's head with his palm. 'I escort your guest to you, Fürst,' the Finder said. 'And now, Göbel, come, it is time for your lesson.' The girl's lovely eyes grew wide and she held fast to the Fürst's gray robe.

" 'It is time, Göbel.'

"The Fürst looked away and said, 'Go, my daughter, you must.' Shoulders bowed, her arms limp, Göbel rose. Hornberg nodded, clutched her elbow and led her from the room and into the darkening corridor.

"The Fürst appeared to have forgotten Schamir and Schamir stood in silence. Of a sudden the Fürst turned to Schamir and said, 'My village is a graveyard where demons dance. I am a widower. My only daughter is a slave. Help me, Physician, help me.'

" 'I do not understand why it is that in your village those with the falling sickness are burned.'

" 'The Finder Hornberg has learned they contaminate the water, their breath is poisonous, their eyes bewitch, their souls are damned. One night, disguised, Hornberg went forth into the village and entered the home of the young widow of an artisan, a woman he suspected of unholy traffic. Bull horns were strapped to his brow, a bearskin bristled from his body, a begemmed tail hung between his legs. The woman woke, convulsed, and shrieked, "The Prince of Hell, Holy Prince of Hell," and kissed Hornberg's scarlet boot. He needed no more proof. The woman was burned the next afternoon. Thirteen others have met the same death.'

" 'But surely the villagers protest,' exclaimed the Physician.

" 'The more they fear, the more they believe him. The shrewish wife of Guildmaster Shenck confided to Hornberg that her spouse was prone to fits. Poor Shenck was burned. A six-year-old girl confessed to him her mother often fainted but continued to move her lips and make birdlike sounds. Now her mother is ashes. I have no power to interfere.'

" 'But you are the lord of the village,' Schamir said in confusion.

" 'Observe,' said the Fürst in a defeated tone. They walked down the stone corridor. Below the stained-glass window of the chapel Göbel was on her knees before the Finder. 'Repeat it again,' Hornberg commanded. ' "Our F–f–fa–t–ther, who–who aaah—," ' and the emaciated girl made a roar and fell writhing to the cold stone. After a time, bedazed, she assumed a kneeling position.

" 'Pray,' the Finder ordered. The girl stuttered the first word, roared, and fell into a jerking swoon. The Fürst could bear no more. Schamir supported him back to his quarters. 'Now you see. If once I overrule Hornberg, he will expose to the villagers that my only child is possessed and she, like the rest, will be burned.'

" 'Fürst von Kisslegg,' said the Physician, 'I have devoted my youth and middle age to travel and the secrets of metallurgy, the hermetic philosophy, and art. I have journeyed to the mines of Sweden to study rare ores, to Turkey and Tartary, Egypt and Italy. This much I know, the falling sickness is in all men and therefore in all the animate and inanimate world that man sees. The quakings of the earth, the spasms of a dreamstruck dog, the tremblings of grass in the wind, all are but discords in the music of the ganglia. Your guildmaster was not possessed. He suffered merely from the retention of his semen. The fainting mother so unnaturally betrayed was the victim of the accumulation of her vital fluids, fluids discharged in a spate of fits.'

"So gladdened did this fruit of Schamir's lonely travel and contemplation make the Fürst that he proposed a scheme whereby his daughter and Schamir might leave in the darkness. They could find refuge in the ruin of the monastery until Schamir had completely dispersed Göbel's malignant collection of vital fluids. Schamir was persuaded, his mule packed with supplies, and in the night he and Göbel stole from the village.

"The Finder was in a rage the next morning. He ordered the castle and houses searched. Göbel was not to be found. That very day Hornberg discovered four girls, a woman, and the groom to be afflicted with the monstrous disease. A collective burning was set for the following morning. The sun rose, but the six had vanished.

"The number living together with Schamir and Göbel increased. Under Schamir's guidance the people did not speak. Rather, they shared themselves with an integrity, a frequency, an abandon, and in combinations they had hitherto been incapable of imagining. Copulation upon copulation, joy on joy, drove the falling sickness from their minds.

"It was the castellan on the battlement who first spied the smoke of a cooking fire rise from the ruin on the hilltop. Thoughts of advancement swelling his brain, he reported his observation to the Finder. That night Hornberg sent the castellan to the monastery.

"The castellan did not return.

"The following night Hornberg dispatched four armed and trusted informers to investigate.

"Nevermore were they seen in the village tavern.

"Baffled by these disappearances, the Finder gnashed and brooded. In desperation he blackened his face with soot, covered his head with rags, and bent like an aged beggar, he hobbled up the slope. To his surprise he was merrily welcomed to the monastery by the black-bearded castellan. 'Join us, old man, for you have entered Paradise.' The Finder smelled the castellan's breath yet could not detect a trace of wine. A cluster of naked men and women (two of the men Hornberg's recently dispatched informers!) were seated in the remains of the monk's library. Their arms were locked and they swayed back and forth, humming in unison. The groom played hopscotch with two young girls, and Schamir and Göbel were fastened on the vestige of the stone altar, their faces luminous as if in trance or prayer.

"The sky was lightening when the Finder wailed down the slope. His rags fell to the ground and sweat etched the soot on his face.

"Eyes like torches, the Finder screamed into the chamber of

the sleeping Fürst, 'You have deceived me. Göbel has not been sucked into the Underworld. She has escaped with the depraved Physician.'

"The Fürst lowered his head.

" 'So, you have known. You know of all the rest. Doubtless, you have arranged it. You have betrayed me and you shall suffer for it.'

"Before that hour had passed, the bell of the castle tolled and through the streets criers called for assembly. Dawn was breaking when the villagers had sleepily gathered in the courtyard. The Finder, clothed in black from the point of his hood to his toes, addressed them from the topmost step of the castle entrance. 'We know demoniacs are among us. We know Lucifer seizes the mighty as well as the poor. I have learned that Göbel, daughter of our Fürst, is in league with devils, that she blasphemes and cannot complete a prayer, that she performs bodily distortions a tumbler would envy. She, along with some dozen villagers, have vanished. I have learned that they have congregated in the ruin.'

"The Finder pointed menacingly toward the hilltop, where a rising red sun limned the monastery. 'There they foully live. The ruin has become a sanctuary for the disciples of the Prince of Hell. There, all the night and all the day, Lucifer's chief disciple, one Schamir the Physician, architects fiendish ecstasies.' The Finder delineated the abominations he had witnessed. A clamor rose from the people. The more closely Hornberg described the happenings at the monastery, the more unruly the villagers became.

"All at once the castle door opened and the Fürst von Kisslegg in his humble gray robe appeared on the highest step beside the Finder. He held up both his arms for silence. The clamor abated. 'This day I relinquish my castle, my wealth, my village, to the Finder Hornberg. I have conversed with the man called the Physician and know him to be a holy man. He has taught me that the falling sickness is in all men. Its cause is the retention of semen and vital fluids. Henceforth I shall live with my beloved Göbel in the monastery above the village.'

"Proudly he descended the castle steps. His former subjects parted to make a path for him.

"Before he had reached the gate of the castle the old cobbler fell in line behind him.

"And a nimble young chorister.

"And her family.

"The trickle of villagers became a stream, the stream a river, the river a flood. All followed the Fürst up the slope toward the architect of ecstasy. In this manner did the sanctuary absorb the inhabitants of the walled village.

"What became of the Finder Hornberg was not precisely known. Some maintained he lived alone in his castle and screeched threats down the echoing corridors. Some said each midnight they heard him demand one Last Fire and some said it was only the wind. Still others said he had exploded, the victim of a cataclysm, for who, they asked, retained more semen than the Finder? One small group, and Schamir was of them, believed the Finder lived among them now but was so thoroughly purged of his rancorous accumulation of semen as to be unrecognizable.

"Before long such speculations ceased. Bliss has a way of dissolving inquiry.

26 Violence.

I floated through the next day, considering various interpretations and thrilling implications of Banok's tour de force. It was unforseeable then that the most exacting trial of my life would come in the next thirty-six hours. Disruption condensed the Week of Film to one evening session and reduced the Week of Organic Language to a single concentrated hour. Within thirty-six hours, pell-mell, we all (excepting

Vincent and Jesse) were loaded in the station wagon and sedan, on the highway headed north to Maine and the Retreat.

And for me the Week of Film had begun in such tranquillity. Most everything was sedate and lazy. Jesse spent the day on the sand looking out on the cove. There was no flint in her facial expression or tone of voice. She had no need of an actor's range of expression. Along with doubt, false pride, and fear, her will was gone. She agreed readily to do or eat what anyone suggested. I can visualize her now out on the beach in the caramel shade of the hut. Her posture, the primitive hut, the white beach, the blue water—all contribute to a picture that might aptly be entitled, "The Abandonment of the Hunt" or "The Discipline of Desire." Whenever I think of Peace, I think of Jesse Staple.

Lynn formed a sensuous parabola in the rope hammock. Robin napped on her birth-wrinkled stomach (she had held apart her bathrobe one morning so I should view this curious phenomenon) or nursed while Lynn read fashion magazines.

Though at best Dot remained crankily aloof and at worst was foul-tempered, she established an odd friendship with Bayla. The two went everywhere together. Dot found a blue rubber air mattress for Bayla and towed her through the water. They took excursions and were always chattering. They seemed to enjoy each other, and so Ellie was at leisure to sunbathe and ramble along the beach. Since Ellie did not ostensibly participate in the seminars, Banok was forced to approach her through other, more casual channels.

Only Vincent was miserable. He stayed to himself. He did not sit still that whole day, He cooked all the meals. Like a man in drying cement, he paced the patio, fingered the stops on his recorder without blowing it, and played horseshoes. He was the spiritual antithesis of Jesse.

Things went along without friction until late that night. Banok set the projector on an end table by the front entrance and aimed it across the patio. Since I was the tallest, I tacked a bedsheet to the redwood paneling at the opposite side of the patio.

Banok was shirtless and wore dungaree shorts and sandals.

How fit and healthy his body was. Short, brown, and extraordinarily well kept, his athletic physique (save the indigo blot of hair extending from armpit to armpit) more resembled a twenty- than a forty-year-old man's. One lunchtime early in the Week of Dialogue, Banok had asked each of us what design came to mind when we looked at his chest hair: Jesse had said an umbrella, Vincent an echinoderm, Bayla a butterfly, Ellie a heraldic bird, Lynn a bear rug, and Dot an octopus—but to me it suggested something far less literal, an ambiguous insignia, a mark of something, an indefinable force with arms outstretched.

Banok clicked a small reel onto an arm of the projector and threaded the film. Bayla said she wanted to stay up and watch the movies. Vincent wildly objected. Banok saw no reason why Bayla should not see the film. Vincent threatened to leave. Lynn left to answer Robin's howl. The projector was ready. Irate, Vincent nonetheless remained.

Banok made an analogy between the Human Head and the projector. "Since all of Nature is palpable thought, the apparatus that turns the reel, the light that throws the image, and the film itself are all components of the Human Head. The head is a projector casting images on a blank sheet. If the head is sound, it must follow that the world projected onto the white sheet be lovely and united. But one caution: never be imprisoned by the belief that this world cast by your own eye, this world *you* have created, has reality independent of you. If I told you that nightly, a woman imagined a man to slip from her bedroom closet with a drawn revolver, you might reply she suffers from any number of ills. If I added, however, that one morning this woman was actually found sprawled on the carpet beside her bed, slain by the man living in her closet, you should not be appalled. It happens every day. Tonight we are going to flush a would-be killer from his hiding place in Vincent's brain."

Banok snapped off the light by the door and snapped on the projector. He centered the fuzzy countdown on the bedsheet and focused a close-up of Vincent in a tiger-striped cabaña outfit seated on the center cushion of a black divan. The unnatural rapidity of the film exaggerated the savagery with which Vincent sucked smoke from his cigarette. He jerkily glanced left and right, eyewhites flashing, and all the while sucked smoke. The camera drew back and it became apparent that Vincent and his divan were situated inside the beach hut. Vincent swung one leg over the other and bounced the elevated foot. Expectantly, he glanced right and left. He flicked the cigarette into the sand and lit another. After several minutes Lynn approached the stuffed right arm of the divan.

Vincent was oblivious. He anxiously scanned the shoreline. Despite the fact she was naked and extremely pregnant, Lynn was apparently invisible to Vincent. Her stomach was shaped like a Golden Delicious apple with a crown of pubic bristle at its pointed base. She carried three oversized dynamite sticks. She sat beside Vincent and placed the sticks on her lap.

She had been seated but a moment when Dot occupied the left cushion. She wore gray Bermuda shorts and a sleeveless white blouse and she too held three red dynamite sticks. As if responding to a cue, the saboteurs rose and inserted the sticks of dynamite under their respective cushions. Moving backwards toward the camera they unwound the long fuses. They had almost reached the edge of the water when they joined their six strands of fuse into one fat twist. Vincent gesticulated furiously in the background as Dot took a wooden match from the pocket of her Bermuda shorts. Lynn held up the fuse.

At precisely this suspenseful instant, hell broke loose. The front door was pushed violently open. The light overhead was switched on. Beside Banok stood an old and shabby devil in a stained undershirt. Lynn clutched her groggy infant and started to weep.

Vincent watched the flickering bedsheet and said, "Turn off the light, turn off the light."

The unclean intruder addressed Lynn: "I had a hunch I'd find you here." He then imperiously asked Bánok, "What do you plan to do about it?" Banok watched the goblin with intensity and was silent. "Come home with me, Carol Lynn," the hobo said, evading Banok's silence. Lynn did not respond.

"I said, what do you plan to do about it?" he yelled, once more shifting targets. Banok looked as one looked at a tormented beast in captivity—with amazement, curiosity, and not a little pity. The beast hurled himself at Banok, who neither shrank nor tried to defend himself. Banok was struck on the side of his neck. His intent countenance was not altered by the attack but Banok said, "I plan to love her."

The sad creature snatched a fork from the kitchen table and with renewed power flew at Banok. He punched a line of red tineholes into Banok's tanned shoulder. I jumped to my feet to subdue the assailant but Banok waved me away.

The fork bounced at Lynn's feet and he muttered, "Are you coming home?" Lynn turned her back to him. He (her derelict father, I later learned) rushed out the door, slurring some intimidation concerning Lynn's age and the police.

The Week of Film was at an end.

The stillness in the room was severe, the lull between lightning bolt and thunderclap. Through it all Vincent sat unruffled, his legs crossed, his eyes on the yellow square of projector light in the center of the bedsheet. It was as if something was revealed there to Vincent for he radiated the misted bliss of a body electrocuted. Behind him the reel spun and the loose end of the celluloid lashed the air. Dot sighed and examined Banok's wound.

"That's the price," she chortled. "Wherever a great mind utters its thoughts, there is Golgotha." Banok abruptly walked out the sliding doors. Dot had not yet even cleaned the wound. Banok wanted solitude. "That's Heine's, not mine," Dot senselessly shouted through the open glass doors. For regardless who wrote the aphorism, it was now forcefully apposite. I have had my Kreblers and Hamblys. Schamir had his Hornberg. The State of the Hunter. And now Banok was the intended quarry.

27 *As Children.* The violence had put me on edge. Bayla's snore sounded off the patio from Dot's bedroom and I could not fall asleep. I switched on the patio light. Vincent's posture was unchanged on the brick floor. Thinking it best not to interrupt him, I quickly shut off the light and decided to walk the beach.

The night was mellow and the soft constant breeze kept the heat from cloying. The light was deceptive. Though it seemed very bright, I had passed the hut when Banok's voice said, "Edgar, will you join us in an experiment?" He was outstretched beneath the thatch roof. Ellie languidly leaned on a corner post. Before the sun had risen I learned the inmost meaning of hospitality, brotherhood, patience, and forgiveness.

There was an ardor, an urgency in Banok's voice I had not heard before: "It looks like there will be no Week of Organic Language. The atmosphere here is too hostile. So much might have been accomplished."

I told him how terrible I too felt.

"Edgar, do you understand why I am saying these words?"

"I understand what you are saying," I said, mystified.

"No, you misunderstand. I speak in order to curb my desire to touch you, to make love to you. When the hindrance of the *Shroud*'s Language, the Word, is removed, every strand of hair stands on end and clacks with eloquence. Once the ancient Organic Language, the prelapsarian tongue, is reclaimed, then each sound, each gesture, is a mating call." Banok sat and spontaneously offered Ellie his right hand and me his left. He pulled us down on the sand so we formed a triangle. "Tonight, if never again, let the three of us speak the Organic Language."

Should the noded wires of an electrostimulator be planted in all my pleasure zones and a simultaneous flow of current be triggered, the resulting seizure of excitation could not equal the wild

arousals I experienced the next half-hour on that beach. Banok
and Ellie took the first step—they engaged in a lighthearted game
of pattycake. Banok slapped his palms on my chest (my palms
had not been ready to meet his) and we started to laugh. We
put our heads together and I felt Banok and Ellie's backs. Hands
rubbed over me. My sensations were raw and young. Banok
kissed me on the throat. There followed a great deal of motion,
tender rubbing and squealing and grunting and growling. It was
difficult to see exactly what was happening. I do remember my
lips pressing Banok's fork wound, the taste of his blood, the smell
of Ellie when she is excited. We three wrestled ourselves into
knots. Banok kicked off his dungaree shorts. Ellie pulled her
jersey over her head and shook her hair. She wore no bra. She
furled off the panties of her bathing suit. Without hesitation I
undressed and, naked, rounds of wrestling and rubbing were gid-
dily resumed. Banok in the middle, we slaphappily rushed the
ocean.

We had become as children. We splashed and touched and
hugged and tittered. I swallowed some saltwater and they
slapped and pounded my back. We high-stepped from the water
in a chain and galloped up and down the beach. We rolled over
and under the sand. I was frenzied. My heart throbbed dizzily
between my ears. It was difficult to see. I was on my stomach
finally, gasping, and hanging onto the instep of Banok's left foot.
My erection had collected a prickly coat of sand.

When I gained sufficient equilibrium to lift my head I saw the
heels of Ellie's feet support her buttocks on either side of Banok's
thighs. He lay on his back. She straddled him, her spine straight,
and he steered her to and fro with hands belted around her
pelvis.

The mind has techniques to deaden such a jolt. Chief of these
is abstraction. I transformed them into a three-dimensional perpendicular. I transformed them into a game of horseshoes: the
iron stake penetrated the U—a ringer, that was all.

But once Banok's legs began to twitch with the galvanic life
of a frog dissected in an experiment, abstraction shattered to

smithereens. Unintentionally I was kicked in the temple. It was then too that Ellie began a series of stertorous yelps, noises she had never made in my bed. Banok rolled on top of her. Ellie hitched her ankles over the small of his sandpapered back. Stormily they commingled and I pushed my face into the sand. It had happened so fast.

Banok had put me to the final test.

I thought of that man Banok once knew, the man totally rid of the *Shroud*. His hospitality. His forgiveness. Not weakness but Vision. Does the thumb possess the forefinger? Is the capillary jealous of the artery?

When once again I raised my head, I saw through a reconstructed eye. Two feet away I saw not the fornication of adulterers, but an extension of my own being. Their climaxes were my climaxes, their satisfactions mine. And when after an eternity they came apart and lay drenched in absolute exhaustion, I likewise lay spent and panting. Banok reached out and squeezed my hand. He understood what had happened. He knew that I too had shared at the last.

Three lovers slept the serene renewing sleep which comes only after perfect lovemaking. My demon of mistrust and watchfulness had been exorcised forever. Since the day of my marriage, I had suspected Ellie of countless furtive copulations. On how many occasions had she taken an extra hour for errands, how many afternoons collected wildflowers in the Maine woods? The pocked youth who packed groceries and carried them to her waiting car? The insolent peachfuzzy lad who delivered a rolled newspaper each dawn while I dozed and returned to collect at dusk when I was away? The game warden she met by the Jack-in-the-pulpit on the rim of a bog? I had never been certain Who, If, and How Many. Not once had I obtained ocular proof. Not even with Krebler. And now on a warm beach in Florida I had come face to face with the elusive male who in manifold guises had cuckolded me for over a decade and I knew him to be myself!

The sky was pale green, the sun yet to rise, when Banok awoke and said, "That was lovely, Edgar." Ellie slept in a curl by his opposite side. I was cramped. Banok scratched sand from his hair, and brushed his naked limbs. We bathed in the ocean, and together dressed in the thatch hut. Banok shook out Ellie's bikini bottom and jersey, tossed it beside her, squeezed saltwater from his black hair and combed it straight back with his fingers. "Only when you are totally rid of the *Shroud* will you always be free to speak the Organic Language you spoke last night," said Banok.

I stated my willingness to do whatever it took.

"Not now, not here," said Banok sadly. "Hostility has poisoned Ponce Beach. Lynn's father is a cruel and dangerous man. No, we must search for a benign environment, a place conducive to the task before you."

In a flash, I thought of the Retreat. My proposal met all the requirements. I told Banok how the vacationers migrated to their cities after Labor Day and the lake offered its beauty and privacy; I described High House, where I might pursue my work in isolation, a monastery far from the walled village. Banok was exuberant. He pressed my body to his.

The sun was ricocheting off the molten cove and we greeted it with a kind of primitive jig. He woke Ellie with the news. She was stunned, dropped her head back on the sand, and laughed like a fool.

Banok packed the station wagon and his sedan with terrific energy. I wired Hambly to prepare the Retreat for our arrival. Ellie and Dot and Bayla took the sedan. Lynn held Robin in the front seat of the station wagon, I stretched in the back, Banok drove.

Before we pulled from the Tarbell driveway, Dot hollered, "What about Vincent and Jesse?"

"They have forgiven themselves," said Banok. "I think they are now ready to respond to one another. Look." Banok pointed to the tableau on the beach.

And that is my final impression of the days at Ponce Beach: Jesse continued to sit under the thatched roof and look out to sea. But the picture "The Abandonment of the Hunt" had an addition—Vincent relaxed in the orange canvas deck chair and played his recorder to her. I could hear the music faintly. He played as naturally and simply as the eloquent wind, one pure prolonged note at a time.

28 Visitation.

Leaking rainwater made a yellow blot on the calcimined ceiling above my head this morning, but I failed to recognize it for what it was, an augury of nightmare. The hair plaster caught the rain and sagged. I moved my slant-top desk from under the enlarging blot and paid it no more attention.

The morning rain changed to a brief hailstorm and the hail softened into the first snow. At the start the snow had melted when it touched the witchgrass and wet milkweed stalks, but by noon, when I went outside for a log to stoke the woodstove, a half-inch had gathered on the fuzzy-looking field and there were no more logs on the porch.

I smiled at the nuisance. A moment before I had been perspiring in the station wagon, readying to speed northward in the September heat, and now I was shivering in slush and snow. The way the brain worked, able to switch seasons in a wink; really, it made no sense. One could get pneumonia.

I tucked Lynn's scarf around my throat and pulled on a turtleneck sweater. I jerked the axe from the block and set out across the orchard in search of wood. There was no wind. Light snow fell straight down. The air was gauzy and gray but I could see to the edge of the orchard. One apple tree had toppled beside a stand of spruces and two others had large arthritic limbs bent down in the snow. At the sound of my axe blade striking into the hard apple wood, a raven rose up from the spruces and lighted on a topmost spruce shaft. The shaft bowed and the raven fluttered and shifted.

My axe bounced off the sinews of the dead apple limb.

A second raven flapped from the spruce stand and settled on the same drooping shaft as the first. Their dark-huddled shapes stayed on, mute in the snowfall.

I dragged one limb across the field to High House porch. The ravens had gone when I returned. But no sooner did I begin to hack at the toppled apple tree than the r-r-r-r-rrk of the obscene couple gargled down from the shaft atop the spruce. So I had interrupted them. I thrust my axe into the trunk and walked into the fragrant stand to investigate. Little snow had gathered on the ground beneath the spruce boughs.

My nose detected the stench, like a fist in the stomach, before the hind legs of a deer jutting from behind a black spruce trunk caught my eye. Only pointed black hooves and the eleven-point antlers were intact. The buck's spine was twisted so the front legs pointed in the opposite direction from the hind legs. The putrefaction had evidently been accelerated by the rains, the feasting of foxes and more recently, the ravens. A well had been opened in the buck's flank and his innards picked and reeled out. Red flakes of meat were scattered around the rim of the gaping gray flank where the ravens were eating. I poked a stick at the haunch in an effort to locate a bullethole but the flesh was too far gone and came apart.

Perhaps Hambly had told me the truth after all. One could hardly determine death cause from the buck's present condition. He might have been killed in another manner. Died of age, parasites; killed by a bobcat or dogs. When I was a boy, Father, Hambly, and I came upon a doe minutes after a dog pack finished. Chunks had been gouged from her hind legs. Her rump and flag were fringed with white and blue cords, vessels, and black streamers. Still, unbelievably, she was alive. Hambly had cursed the dogs, shot the doe behind her wide-open eye, and field-dressed her. Who could say this had not happened to the buck? Dogs. Hambly could have lied. A coincidence. A deer can die so many ways in the woods.

I chopped wood without pause and by the early darkness had

stacked a week's firewood on the porch. The wet apple wood
was difficult to start in the stove. I splintered a cupboard shelf
for kindling and boiled rice, the remaining dried figs, and sliced
apples into the same pot. I scanned the account of my confrontation with Hambly. His indictment, "You're the bootcher, Edgar,
not me," strikes me as singularly hateful. Even if Hambly had in
fact wounded the buck, I could not have backed down. Concepts
Hambly could never comprehend, issues of far greater importance
than a deer, were at stake. A line had to be drawn somewhere.
If I *had* permitted Hambly to trail the buck he had wounded or
fabricated, he was sure to have returned to kill more.

I finished supper and grabbed the teakettle to fill it in the
spring. I opened the front door and tensed from head to foot.
"Oooh-a-a-aarh" screeched a stooped purple-headed form on the
porch. Dot held open a burlap sack and said, "Trick or treat."
She folded the purple knit snowcap up over her gold-wire glasses
and said, "Don't be spooked, Edgar, it's Hallowe'en," and gruffly
laughed by herself. "Come on, help me with this bundle. I'm the
one who lugged it up the hill and it's for you." Her nose and
cheeks were orange and her eyes teared from the cold. I carried
the burlap sack into the room and heaved it on my bed.

"I haven't seen any snow for five years, you know," said Dot
stamping her boots. "Not since Banok taught in Canada. Never
snows in Southern California and Acapulco or on the Gulf. Five
years."

She shook the snow like dust from her cap, mantled her coat
over the stool, and wiped steam from her glasses. She warmed
herself beside the woodstove while I pumped the gas lamp
brighter and unloaded a bag of potatoes, onions, canned peas,
beans, okra, prunes, four boxes of elbow noodles, a small wheel
of cheddar cheese, two heads of lettuce, a squashed carton of
tomatoes, eight rolls of toilet paper, and a gallon of fuel for the
gas lamp. "I appreciate this, Dot, it's just that you startled me.
You should have waited until daylight."

"Hallowe'en comes only once a year. I had to get out and scare
the hell out of you. I didn't think any kids would drop by up

here and I hated the thought of you waiting for somebody all night behind the door with a full box of candy in your hands." She winced and inhaled dramatically. "What do you do in here, shit on the floor?"

I averted my face and explained, "It's gotten so cold outside, I made an opening in the pantry floor. I can't smell it. I should get lime to sweeten it."

"Fine thing," Dot said, flexing her brow in censure or mock censure. I assorted the goods and arranged them on the floor by the wainscoting. "How's your notebook coming?" she asked, a question detonating such a flurry of answers I could only take my notebook from the desktop and hand it to her.

My first reader leafed casually through my careful pages. Some pages had been ripped out and every page has words scrawled, words laboriously crammed above and below lines and in columns. "Rough draft, all right," was her sole critique. "How far have you gotten?"

"I'm nearly caught up with the present," I said.

"What do you plan to do when you've gone full circle, keep a diary?"

"I'm not certain." It was an ugly question. "Possibly I'll come back down. I haven't thought about afterward."

"Well, you can always make up things. I don't see much difference between describing something that's happened to you and something that might happen to you or somebody else," said Dot, sketching the outlines of her rudimentary aesthetic.

"It seems to me matters of style and the serious matter of reconstructing oneself make grotesque bedfellows," I pleasantly remembered. "I'm not here to make up stories. I'm here to save my life." I jabbed a log into the red coals and asked if there were any new developments about the school.

Dot smirked dejectedly and sat on the down quilt at the foot of the bed. She looked at the link of diagonals on the wainscoting. "I think you and me are in the same boat, Edgar."

"It will take an enormous effort just to prune the orchard, let alone restore this farm, but if children and painters and musicians will all —" I cut myself short. Dot did not seem to follow. If she didn't know about the planned school, Banok had reasons. He was not a haphazard man.

"Will all what, Edgar?"

"Learn," I said evasively.

"Screw," said Dot brutally. "Don't mince. Intellectual fucking, that's what they'll do."

"I'm sorry for you, Dot," I confessed.

Dot exhaled a violent whistle through her teeth and rose off the bed. Brusquely, she jammed on her purple cap and coat. The tears I saw run between her cheeks and nostrils so shocked me, seemed so alien to her abrasive nature, I swallowed my philosophic and aesthetic antagonisms and said, "Please, Dot, it's Hallowe'en. I'll open the can of plums and we can have tea."

She halted by the door and rigidly wagged her head left and right as if she were about to cross a busy street. She laughed suddenly and rubbed fingers under her glasses. I took possession of her coat and hat and laid them on my pillow. My mind swirled from her outburst. Dot was out of character. I ransacked my shrunken inventory of openings appropriate to a civil chat.

"Skip the plums," Dot said, "tea will be fine." I took the kettle and said, "I was on my way to the spring when you ambushed me. I'll be right back."

From across Rust Lake a wind slanted the fine snow. Three inches had accumulated. I scooped the cold water into the kettle and hesitantly returned. "This is a regular blizzard," I chatted, setting the hissing kettle on the woodstove. "You'll be wishing you hadn't seen snow for five more years before the spring."

"I like winter."

"I wasn't even aware that Banok ever taught in Canada," I said, shoved a knobby chunk of apple wood into the stove, and slammed the door with my boot toe. "Sure you don't want plums?"

"Positive."

I opened the can and sat on the edge of my bed, forking plums and sipping the rich juice. "I certainly can't imagine Banok at a college," I inquired delicately, clearing syrup from my throat. The kettle began to steam and I sprinkled herbs in a cup and set it on the desk for Dot.

"How do you imagine him?" grinned Dot.

"No way in particular. Truthfully, it's difficult to picture him as a child with parents or married to a wife. It has nothing to do with you, Dot. It's uncanny, like some kind of aura. As if he had no past life. As if Banok were always present tense." I tried to conceal my satisfaction with that last phrase, while Dot drank tea and blinklessly considered me.

"You really mean it, don't you?" she said.

"I do," I said.

"If you knew all the other submissions, commitments, and sincerities your words bring back, Edgar. And their results."

I pressured her with expectation of an explanation. An intense gloom was at work to catch hold of me.

"You know, Edgar, it's a funny thing, but despite my own humiliations and the brains I've seen fill up with the holy helium of abstractions and rise to altitudes where all things pop, I love Banok too."

Dot ignored me now. She studied the dregs of her teacup, as if a tiny script were submerged there: "I loved him when he was an associate professor in Ontario, and I suppose I even love him now, years after his literary conversion. He taught up there the first eleven years we were married. Up until his sabbatical he gave a course called 'Sinking as a Fine Art.' He published a few articles and lectured on Wit and Decorum, couplets, Nature, Reason, Deism . . . the usual. The course wasn't too popular so he spent the whole year of the sabbatical looking over the fence at the other side of the century, the greener side, he might say, and when Banok leapt that fence, he went head first. Chatterton led him to Macpherson, Macpherson to Blake and Smart. Hazardous men," Dot said, exposing her top teeth, "but most hazardous when read for advice on how to live, for an exit, or a launch. In a year or two our discouraged associate professor was a fullblown Bible musician and his course 'The Oracular Voice' was the most popular on the campus. Instead of the topiary at Twickenham, Banok talked about Vision and the Apocalypse when all nature would blossom into human life."

Dot's voice had grown so exultantly bitter, I stood up to protest, but her voice rose and denied me. "And not only in the classroom. Everywhere. He began to insist I have relationships with other men or, if I wanted, women. He said I must have the freedom to love. He made me feel like I was diseased, that I stood for Death, and he was fighting for Life; that I was Morality, Security, and Fear, he was Instinct. He suggested all kinds of arrangements. I don't even think it was because he was having some affair and felt guilty."

"What did you say?"

"I told him I didn't want to have a lover."

"Because you were afraid?" I suggested.

"Because I loved him."

Possessiveness. Dot had been unable to keep pace with Banok's development. "And why do you think he wanted you to take lovers?"

"I know why. For his Idea. For the principle of it."

"And you don't agree?"

"Fucking for metaphysics?" she laughed caustically. "Let me tell you about that, Edgar. He got so bad he threatened to leave me five years ago, can you believe it, leave me, if I wouldn't cooperate with his vision and have an affair. I couldn't stand it. And one afternoon in the spring I gave in. Banok had a class that evening. So I walked right up to Gregory Mott, a bald chemist, a bachelor in a bulky cardigan and tight shiny-black pants, and I actually pleaded with him to come to our house, screw me, and save my marriage. The rest of the day we drank, vodka, we got drunk, and he talked about this hamster-breeding project that a fat girl and a scrawny boy charted in the basement of the chemistry building. He put on a violin concerto of Mozart and described how they chronicled those hamster matings and held hands; how they named the adult hamsters and all their numerous offspring. And all the while Mott was ensconced on our sofa in his underwear, snickering and drinking vodka to Mozart with his free hand plumbing under my skirt. He wanted all the lights on in the bedroom. He lay down on top of me and poked and scratched and pressed and without either entering or I think even achieving an erection, came off on the sheet and passed out. I heard the apartment door open and made believe I was asleep. The bedroom lights were all shut off. We were covered with a sheet like we were a couple of corpses. Mott flopped over on Banok's side of the bed. The instant Mott revived, Banok greeted us from the doorway with a tray of fresh coffee."

"So Banok was the man," I burst with the glee of discovery. I leafed through my book and aloud read, " 'I once knew a man, a teacher, totally rid of the *Shroud*. He returned home one chilly night and discovered his wife with her lover, asleep in the bedroom. A light was on and nothing covered their nakedness. So banal, this situation is nonetheless archetypal, the touchstone of countless philosophies, murders, jests, and novels. But the man I knew spread a sheet and blanket over the exhausted lovers' bodies so they would not be cold. He turned off the lights so they should sleep well. That evening he prepared refreshments for them. This was not weakness but Vision.' That's Banok, the man totally rid of the *Shroud* IS Banok."

"The foul bastard," said Dot leadenly.

"And all these five years you haven't forgiven yourself," I said, bouncing to my feet. The pieces had come together. "For years you have blamed Banok for your *own* feelings of guilt."

"Forgive myself, Edgar? Oh, I forgive myself all right. It's Banok I don't forgive. He hasn't slept with me since that night. Not touched me these five years."

Shaken, unclear as the pieces blasted apart, I mustered only "You must forgive him."

"Me forgive?" Dot shrieked. "Forgive him when he plows one girl after another right under my nose to show how he despises me?"

"You must."

Dot yanked on her hat and coat. "You forgive him. Forgive him for your wife, Edgar."

"You can't comprehend that," I exclaimed.

"Then forgive him for screwing Bayla. That should take some forgiving."

My blood became Novocain. "You lie," I said gently, "you tell lies."

Dot trembled and slowly she turned, opened the front door, and walked off the porch into the slanting snow. She had walked ten steps and was gone from my sight. I sadly recalled Bayla's yellow slicker retreating in the drizzle. I slammed the door and leaned upon it. She lies, I thought. She's mad.

Instantly it struck me that Dot's visit had been but a maleficent imagining. But the empty plum can on the floor, her tea-cup, the fresh supplies said it had not. Such was her jealousy, her resentment of Banok's affection for me, she schemed to set one against the other. Perhaps Banok had sent Dot to High House to try the outermost limits of my loyalty. Dot lies. She is a jester, a troublemaker. Trick or treat! A Hallowe'en trick? She is deranged. Why Bayla is not yet a full-grown woman. So far as I know she has yet to have her first flow. She is after all just twelve years old. But Bayla is most mature for her age. And I have not been close to her, not as I should have been. Dot's account of her infidelity with the chemist did coincide with Banok's man who was rid of the *Shroud*. Yet, if she told the truth. My only child. My daughter. The fork wound. Retribution. What do you plan to do about it? If it is true, if it is, and Banok has deceived me, then I grasped the handle of the gas lamp and like Urizen exploring his dens, like lunatic Diogenes, I staggered past the plastic curtain into the cold stinking pantry. Gaslight illuminated the small room. I regarded the dismantled cupboard, pulled down my pants, and squatted. My buttocks hung over the hole in the pine floor. Horror, uncertainty, and plums had done their work.

29 I tried a walk this afternoon to gather my thoughts, but thoughts would not cohere. The low sky was thick and gray and appeared static. The snowfall has stopped but not the wind. Half a foot of loose snow has drifted against the apple tree trunks. The base of the woodpile on the porch is covered. A tiny drift has settled by the axe blade sunk in the chopping block. I walked the perimeter of the orchard. The cold wind made my forehead hurt more. As I skirted the stand of spruce where yesterday I chopped wood, the frigid sheen of ravens rose to a sprucetop. They screeked down at me like noisemakers, party favors, and looked elsewhere. I trod through the snow to High House. I attempted to read this notebook, from the beginning.

30 I tried to continue my story tonight. It must be past midnight now and still I can't bring myself to permit the two vehicles to leave the horseshoe drive of the Tarbell Ranch.

Vile thoughts proliferate like fruit flies. "What do you plan to do when you've gone full circle, keep a diary?" This is the vilest question of all. The circle is nearly complete.

Then what? Then my next sentence must be preceded by some event, some action; the next sentence, persistent as the clink of this winter fly on my windowpane, will be always a step behind me and I will have to keep moving or there will be no more sentences, nothing more to describe.

"You can always make up things," Dot had said. But if ever it comes to that, to lying, I will be lost. I would become the *Shroud* itself and the Third Step, the *Holy Androgyne*, nothing but a tormenting vision of the lowest depth of ocean, a frigid place where no light reaches and skeletal phosphorescent fish are welded together, male and female, for propagations.

No alternative remains but to go down and ask Banok, point blank, for the truth.

31 *Leviathan Porcupine.* I tied Lynn's orange and brown scarf around my throat, tucked its fringed tips beneath my shirt, pulled on the heavy turtleneck, draped the mackintosh poncho over my head, and stepped into that midnight. Before I had reviewed my decision to question Banok, I was plunging between the apple trees. Soft flakes, slow and far apart, fell to the ground. From the spruce boughs snow tumbled and thudded like books knocked off a shelf. The snow had not drifted on the ridgeside as in the orchard and I slowed to a crunching walk. I descended the dark slope in such an oblivion that the Retreat (chimney smoking and its windows hazily aglow like a woodcutter's cozy cottage in fairytales) startled me to a halt.

The night was so silent I could hear snowflakes hit the hood of my poncho. I shook my head as if to ward off some powdery spell, peered through the window into the empty downstairs, marched to the front of the Retreat, and twice grazed my knuckles on the storm door. Snowflakes dissolved in my hot beard. I waited, knocked louder and louder, and was about to pound again, when, dismayed, I realized I was beating upon my own door. I flung the door open.

"Oh, it's you, Edgar," Lynn cried, wrapped in a white Hudson's Bay blanket at the top landing. "I thought I heard something." Holding the rail, Lynn pattered sluggishly downstairs and hugged my wet poncho. Her blanket slid to the floor. I stomped my boots on the hearth and Lynn, wearing only sheer sky-blue underpants, stooped to retrieve the blanket, wound herself in it, and sank into the wicker rocker before the burned-down black and orange fire. "What's wrong?" she asked, "You look bad."

I watched her in a noncommittal way, to trap her. "What do you mean?"

"What time is it? What's happened?"

"You tell me, Lynn."

She stroked her forehead with her fingerpads, spasmodically took in air, and yawned profusely. "Where is everyone?" I said, nearing her rocker. The heat drove me away. I stripped off my slick poncho and sweater, purposely left Lynn's scarf around my neck, and carried an oak chair beside her.

Over the mantel, I noticed the old snapshot of my family in the canoe. It had been a mistake that day, perhaps a telltale mistake, to surrender the stern and only paddle to Ellie.

I remembered the day Banok nodded at the dead buck in the older photograph, the first deer I ever killed. "Did you shoot this?" he had taunted. I should have described how I tracked him half a day in snow and mud, how three or four times I sighted him without taking off the safety, how I didn't want to shoot him so much as follow his deep crescent-moon hooves in the crystal mud of dark cedar swamps, trailing his jagged line of broken snowcrust up a juniper meadow to the bristled spine of a ridge. The tracks entered a pine thicket where I discerned the flicker of an ear. My fingers were frosty and dull in my gloves and I fired quickly. Momentarily, the buck bolted from the pines, bounded into the air, and jabbed his dead snout into the snow as if some second infallible and silent bullet had hit mark. I had bawled. It wasn't the sudden gracelessness of the dead deer, the reddening snow melting from the hot blood and body, or the long difficult drag to Retreat which grieved me. I wept because it had been a pleasant adventure to follow the meandering tracks wherever they decided I should follow. There was no path left to follow; the trailmaker himself was no more; the quest was over.

I gazed at the red chips in the firebox, redolent once more of Blakean musclemen roasting in pointy flames, and I shifted in my chair, noticed the puddle of melted snow at my feet, and sharply asked, "Is Banok upstairs?"

Her chair rocking like a metronome, Lynn nodded. The most enervating of possibilities occurred to me: that I had yet to *begin* my period of isolation, that the past five weeks at High House were the creation of one tortuous night of insomnia, that shortly Lynn was to congratulate me on my courage, express her hope that Robin, when self-sufficient, would follow in my footsteps, and I would have to start on my solitary journey all over again.

The quandary which motivated my descent had begun to lose its intensity. Without a spur to action, I knew I would skulk to the door and climb the ridge, wondering if Lynn would think on my visit as a dream, and hoping enough snow would fall to fill my boot tracks to High House. So I pressed on, leaning on the arm of my chair to whisper, "To your knowledge, Lynn, has Banok had intercourse with my daughter?"

Lynn's head was slung toward me. Her hair hung in a mustard curtain to the floor. I rose to take a closer look. As if astounded, Lynn's long mouth gaped, but her eyes were shut tight.

Red sparks buzzed, jigged, and extinguished on the stone hearth when I dropped a log on the grate and straightened it with the poker. With a dread raging like hives I walked upstairs, switched on the fluorescent halo of hall light, and opened the door to the master bedroom.

The finger of light which streaked toward the bed indicated Banok, battleship gray and very straight, his fingers interlocked over his navel like some effigy atop its ancient sarcophagus. Ellie was swaddled in a hump of blanket, quilt, and pillow at the edge of the brass bed.

I made a cautious step forward and heard, "Edgar" in the objective and peculiar voice of an usher paging during performance, a secretary announcing a name in a doctor's waiting room.

"I need to speak with you, Banok," I said. With a garble and then a loud tremulous hoot, Ellie sat up. "What do you want?" she asked uneasily, as if recollecting the mortification to which the *Shroud* had subjected her on the night of my waking vision.

In reply to Ellie's initial owlish whine, a high-pitched howl and hoot sounded in the hallway. Steadfast, I said, "I want to speak with Banok."

"Certainly," agreed Banok. He hopped from bed, dipped into the closet, and buttoned a beige trenchcoat up his chest hide.

The hall jerked and fluttered with commotion like the corridor of a moving train. A specter in a white blanket, Lynn swished past me and on toward the howling guestroom. Dot's belligerent head poked out of Bayla's compartment to shout "Quiet" and whisper "You're a sore sight." Banok tapdanced down the stairs and I, for bearing, braced myself on the pine-paneled wall as Lynn hustled Robin downstairs.

Banok had poured himself a glass of milk and settled in a ladderback chair at the round table. He invitingly patted the chair beside him. The tan was gone from his swarthy olive-colored face. His enormous dilated eyes appraised me. "Sit down, Edgar, what's wrong?" Again he stiffly patted the empty seat.

"What has happened to *you?*" I replied.

"What the hell is this?" bellowed Dot on her way down.

"I don't understand," said Banok, "Dot told us . . ."

"I told them the sorry truth, Edgar, that it stunk to high heaven up there." Dot grinned. Her face offered me no private message, nothing but Dot the old Leg-Puller. I had no idea how to start and I was fast losing a reason why. "I found this deer in the woods," I said.

"Found?" said Banok, perplexed.

"It was rotten. Hambly killed it, I think."

"But he was forbidden to hunt," said Banok.

"I know that but I . . . but then, Dot scared me on Hallowe'en."

"She said that," Banok smiled. "She said you were doing fine work."

"She did?" I was drifting.

"Edgar, you know what secret thoughts can do. A hidden thought becomes a quill of Memory, have you forgotten? Open your hands to us, what is it?" Banok stood, reached two fists toward me, rolled them and sprung open his fingers, smooth palms up. "My hands are open, Edgar, are yours?"

On the stairway Ellie snapped. "What is this nonsense? Who can sleep?"

"I would prefer to talk to Banok alone," I said.

"If we allow closed hands now, Edgar, we have failed."

I looked down at his short bushy legs under the hem of his trenchcoat and blurted, "Have you touched Bayla?"

"Often," said Banok immediately as he sat down, "I do often."

"Intimately," I pushed myself to say.

"Did Dot say that to you?" asked Banok wearily. And of all things he took Dot's hand and appeared to lightly squeeze it. It was the only contact I ever saw between them.

"How I know is inconsequential," I said. "I want the truth from *you*."

"Dot," said Banok abruptly, "bring Bayla down here."

"NO," stormed Ellie, blocking the stairway. "What is this, a goddam court?"

Banok saw Ellie was adamant, paused, made a megaphone of his hands, threw back his head, and three times shouted "Bayla." "If you have such suspicions, doubting Edgar, question your daughter directly."

This I neither expected nor wanted. Bayla appeared at last in green pajamas, and puffy and squinting from the light, she shuffled downstairs and past her enraged mother.

"Hello, Bayla, I've missed you," I began, and kissed her sweaty head. "How are you?"

"Sleepy," she whined, "I want to go to bed," and she tossed herself onto the burgundy fainting couch.

"Honey," I said quietly, sitting beside her, "I want to ask you one very important question, and then you can go right back to bed."

"Shut up, Edgar," commanded Ellie. It was an awkward moment. I did not know how to phrase the question. "Bayla," I asked as kindly as I could, "has Banok ever touched your privates?"

"Oh my God," exclaimed Ellie.

Bayla wrinkled her mouth and rolled over on the couch. I massaged her shoulder to try to put her at ease and said, "Has he . . . did he ever try to feel below your waist?" Bayla turned to me, a look of fierce confusion on her face. Her lower lip trembled, and shaking her head faster and faster so her hair swatted one side and the other, she started to weep. Ellie took Bayla's arm, shuddered, and hurried away from me, and upstairs.

I had committed myself and was doing badly. Angered, I walked to the round table and demanded that Banok himself tell me the truth. He watched me mercilessly and said, "How can there be such a thing as truth in an atmosphere of antagonism and mistrust?"

"I have no antagonism," I said, "I only wanted to find out."

"That you must do so is a measure of your failure, my own, all of ours. Our garden, our school, the entire venture here at the Retreat has failed."

"What do you mean. All because I ask one question?"

"Because you have not learned to draw a clear line, Edgar." Who was this swarthy squareheaded man with hot saturnine eyes, a cleft nose, and thick lower lip? The ill-proportioned martinet I then saw propped in the ladderback chair was a perfect stranger. "You're not Banok," I accused him.

"Edgar," he said, "sit down, calm yourself."

"You're an imposter."

"Imposter?" he frowned, fins of black hair jutting over his ears. "Edgar, tonight you remind me of the man who entered his living room and discovered a small fox gnawing into the seat of his favorite armchair. This fox was manifestly ill. His coat was bedraggled and yellow, but he bore none of the earmarks of a deranged animal."

"Not this way," I pleaded.

"No excessive salivation."

"Simply state the truth."

"No spastic movements."

"Yes or no," I begged, my head depressed in my hands.

"On the contrary, Edgar, this fox was strangely at ease. The man backed to the closet and fetched the loaded pistol he kept there. He crept behind the fox, aimed at the base of the fox's skull, and was pressuring the trigger when the fox gave him a swift disdainful glance and said in a clotted voice, 'Do you always react like this?'

" 'But rabies reports are everywhere,' the man reasoned, humiliated. 'The Veterinarian in Charge of Animal Disease, the Livestock Specialist, and the Director of Animal Industry jointly attribute the disease to you, the red fox.' The frightened man went on to describe the needle treatment administered one bitten by a rabid red fox.

"The fox snorted, and resumed burrowing into the man's favorite armchair. Balls of stuffing piled on the floor. The man considered the cunning of the Fox, how foxes had been known to lure pursuing hounds to their deaths on railroad trestles, how, in fable, the credulity of the Crow had proven fatal.

" 'You think this is a ruse, eh?' said the fox. 'Believe me, we foxes are hard put to live up to our age-old reputations. These days, if we so much as pirouette, somersault, or romp about, if a fox goes on a spree, kicks up his heels, suddenly the whole race of foxes is rabid.'

"It was the threat of those immense needles lanced through his navel or thereabouts, the excruciating pain of rabies treatment, which induced the man to pull the trigger at last. He drove the dead fox to the laboratory of the Veterinarian in Charge of Animal Disease, but owing to the fox's badly mutilated brain, the examiner was unable to determine if the fox was rabid or not. He termed the result of the biopsy 'inconclusive.' "

Banok made no effort to protect himself. He toppled as the ladderback chair toppled. My knee pinned the epaulet of his trenchcoat, my fist gripped one of the unfurled black wings of hair on the side of his head, and repeatedly I witnessed his impassive but resilient skull bounce on the hardwood floor when, far away, I heard Ellie's tightened voicebox issue one word, "FAGGOT," felt a tattoo of pain expand my head, and there was darkness, absolute darkness.

My eye sockets were dead with cold, my neck muscles were locked, and my stomach was clenched and bitter when I revived. Behind my lids, green dots glowed, blinked, and glowed like cold luminous abdomens of lightning bugs along a black woods path. I opened my eyes to escape, but saw the dreadful green constellations those fish employ in their heatless antilight to woo prey and paramour alike.

It had happened, I thought. I had become the *Shroud*.

My fingers frantically searched out and seized the freezing compress on my eyes and brow; I sat up; the contents of my head sloshed noisily, and I eased back down. Gradually, I recognized the feel of the burgundy fainting couch beneath me. I heard a hiccough and thick sniffle and the rumble of a fire. Something extraordinary had occurred to punish my head and so utterly boggle its contents. The severest pain seemed to radiate icicles from my cowlick. Where a rounded scalp had lately been, my thumb and forefinger explored horrid boulders, eskers, drumlins. I lifted my head and tugged out an ice-pack in a yellow blood-smudged towel.

I rolled my raw glacier-scoured head toward the warm blue aura of burning logs, the vermiculate mantel, and with an ugly jolt I noticed beside the photograph of my first trophy nothing but a black-framed square of blank cardboard.

I strained to sit. There in the corner was Lynn's pinched and trembling face, her small eyes popped in such alarm they might have been chosen from the glossy rows of a taxidermist's cabinet. "Lynn?" I called.

Robin hiccoughed in her lap and Lynn wailed, "What am I supposed to do? I'm broke and I can't go back to Florida, not ever," and she dwindled to a silent sobbing.

"What happened to my head?"

"I thought sure you were killed and that me and Robin were

left behind, alone with a dead man. She beat on your head so hard, the poker prong broke off. Nobody thought about me and Robin. We don't have a penny. Where can I go?"

"Who beat my head?"

"Dot, Dot did. All of a sudden everybody went nuts."

Her hysteria actually absorbed my pain and with care I got to my feet and reached out. "Don't worry," I said, "I have money, I can provide." Lynn shot from her chair in panic, sidled by me, raced upstairs, a slam, and pushed furniture squealed on its way to barricade a door.

I staggered toward the fire and spread my arms along the mantel. I faced the framed cardboard which, so long, provided backing for the photograph of my family. There were no escapes left. I had tried every one. I had longed to soar in the azure liberation of a structured, symbolic vision, but again I had bungled and had to show for all my striving a jumble of roadsigns and symbols which simultaneously directed me up, forward, backward, right, down, and left.

Where had I snagged? Why? I had followed Banok's prescription to the letter. I had patiently suffered the removal of many deep-stuck quills of Memory. I had extracted that blue wing aquiver in a cat's mouth, pulled out a black snorkel spouting salt-water, a game of horseshoes on a sultry shore, an Italian grey-hound dead in a shoebox; I had pried out an inchoate menagerie of worms, crickets, toads, raccoons, mice, a bison, a mongoose, eagles and moles, hares and hounds, porpoises, owls, ravens, deer, oxen, and foxes; I extracted a wide range of heads, beginning with the complex topography of Robin's greased head, the lettuce head my merry assassin of a wife once hacked at the sideboard, a seven-headed prophetic unit, the *Life-size Human Head*, a communal brain of peach stones—and yet, though all these barbs and more had been dutifully sunk into the pages of this note-book, they nonetheless remained lodged in my own beastly sea urchin of a head, a head so riddled with the quills of Memory that to complete an extraction were futile, for life itself was one

Leviathan Porcupine driving home its quills from dawn until dusk, and doubly so in those wretched lonely hours of night.

32 *Thanksgiving.* "FAGGOT," Ellie had branded me, and for weeks afterward I found ample justification for the charge. After all, I had known that Banok was ideologically bound not to defend himself. On one day my craven aggression appeared a cry for intimacy, a confession of loneliness; the next day I was jealous of my daughter, or merely the dupe in Dot's vicious gambit to win back her husband. Another day I believed the whole horror might not have happened if I had eaten something in those thirty hours prior to my descent, if I had not been afraid of the consequences of completing my notebook, if I had comprehended the final parable of the talking fox.

At the end of a week I saw in my assault the Son/Student/Disciple's inevitable rejection of his Father/Teacher/Master. The longer I mulled over motives, the more convinced I became that I belonged with Lynn's fork-brandishing father and all the other Kreblers, hellish Hornbergs, Hamblys, and fox-killers who peopled the treacherous State of the Hunter in the *Shroud's* domain.

To avert the irreversible declaration of self-hatred, I scissored off my hair and beard, but despite a new face, Lynn walked on her toes, an animal in terror. She stayed as close to Robin and as far from me as the walls of the Retreat permitted. She was the first person in many years to be intimidated by me.

Tense silence prevailed until our supplies ran out. That morning I hiked along the icy road to Rust Lake Village and returned with bag upon bag of groceries loaded in the back of a new pickup with a bright orange hydraulic plow.

Lynn helped me unload. A heaping brown bag in each arm,

a terse smile lighting her haggard face, she said, "Thank you, Edgar."

If not for that simple smile and "thank you," the preceding section would never have been written. I could never have retrieved my notebook from filthy High House (the sack of potatoes had been looted, the onions scattered, the lettuce, noodles, tomatoes, and cheese devoured, the toilet paper, even, nibbled). Broken bits of yellow plaster had dropped to the floor beneath the chalky ceiling lathes. Let the *literal* porcupines inherit High House!

It no longer matters to me that, independent of Dot's connivance, Banok may well have been secretly fornicating with my daughter until, penitent, he had related the inopportune fox parable in order to incite my assault; that the whole episode illustrated the Father's impulsive protection of his Child; that the moment I toppled Banok, I reclaimed the stern and paddle of the marriage canoe; that the "Faggot" Ellie called me was a hollow word hurled from the horror and impotence of her vanishing mastery. I am not interested. If he wishes, Ellie's lawyer can make the further inquiries. My time of ruminations and self-investigations is over. Rather than an epilogue to a notebook, I feel confident the present happenings at the Retreat will prove a prologue to a new life.

Myself, I have explored one tiny star in the overlapping, interlocking galaxies of marital metaphysics and the metaphysics of divorce. There are Anemic Marriages, I have heard, in which neither party much affects the other. Common Marriages are plentiful, where one is sapped, the other indifferent; one enriched, the other unaffected. And there are Satanic Marriages such as my late marriage, where Ellie progressively reduced me, was unable to do otherwise, and for a time, flourished.

What is evolving between Lynn and myself at the present time, however, differs from all the above. Her needs are obvious. I can meet them. I, too, have needs. Lynn is no wizard, it is true, but I have not experienced such a renewal of strength since the beginnings of my marriage to Ellie. Lynn depends upon me, and each passing day the dependence deepens. Ours is a relationship in which each is indispensable to the other, a Reciprocal Marriage, it might be called.

Tomorrow is Thanksgiving Day and I have decided once again to eat meat. Lynn had made a loaf of bread shaped like a toadstool and another like a woman's auburn braid. I smell the apple and pumpkin pies in the oven. Stuffed, stitched, and ready for basting, the turkey sits under cheesecloth in the refrigerator.

It is no small pleasure to observe others moving about me as if they recognize my value and what they recognize does not displease them. When Lynn, Robin, and I gather together at the round Thanksgiving table, I will say a special Grace.

To you, Robin, I will give thanks for squeezing pumpkin pulp through your fingers and waxing the floor with it. Thanks for your simple laughter today when you spotted that bully jay chasing off the smaller birds to gobble down all the snow-covered seeds for himself.

Lynn, I will give thanks to you for your white hands folding dough on the butcher block; for the two dark circles your breasts' milk seeped into the front of your blouse while you wrestled with the warps and wefts of your miniature loom.

And I thank you my profoundest thanks, Lynn, for the rediscovery of my courage. Amen.